The Striding Spire

Spire

MODERN MAGICK, 3

CHARLOTTE E. ENGLISH

1

LET'S JUST SAY THAT my first date with Baron Alban did not go quite as I was hoping.

Expectations: me in a *very* good dress. High heels, great up-do, a bit of lipstick (or perhaps a lot). The Baron looking gorgeous as always in one of his many fine suits, escorting me upon one muscular arm to somewhere lovely. Somewhere with music, perhaps, and good cake.

Reality: Somewhat different.

It began with a phone call.

'Morning, Ves,' came the Baron's deep voice when I picked up. 'Do I disturb?'

'Not at all!' said I brightly, and not altogether truthfully. It was, I had blearily noted as I scooped up my phone, all of half past six in the morning; it was Sunday, and I'd had no intention of getting up for at least three hours yet. I was in bed with my duvet around my chin, and the UniPup, all yellow fur and tiny puppy snores, was asleep on my neck. 'What can I do for you?' It wasn't so easy to speak with a weight on my throat. I hoped she would grow out of that habit by the time she grew much bigger.

'We've been talking about going out sometime for a while, and I was wondering — are you busy today?'

'Today?'

'Yes.'

I thought furiously, but only for about two and a half seconds. 'No!' I said with emphasis. I might have been smiling like an idiot, but that I cannot confirm.

'Great!' He sounded happy, too, which I will not deny was good for my ego. 'I'll pick you up in half an hour.'

'*Half an hour*?!'

'Is... that okay?'

I've been on a few dates in my time, and I will be self-aggrandising enough to own that some of those gentlemen were flatteringly eager. But this was something else. 7am on a Sunday morning? Nobody was *that* eager for my company. 'It's fine,' I said, scooping the puppy off my neck. I laid her gently on the pillow next to me — she didn't wake — and stumbled out of bed. 'As long as there is going to be breakfast involved, and soon.'

'That can be arranged. See you soon, Ves.' And he hung up.

Odd.

But with only twenty-eight minutes of the promised half hour left, I had no time to puzzle over it. What did a Cordelia Vesper wear on a shockingly early-morning breakfast date with the handsomest troll alive? *This* Cordelia Vesper had no idea, and she'd have to figure it out pretty fast.

I MADE IT DOWN to the hall with exactly thirty-seven seconds to spare. With May dawning dewily outside, the day promised to be warm and fine, so I had chosen one of my favourite dresses — a knee-length confection of red viscose, printed with roses — and thrown a light cardigan over it. My trusty hair-fixing Curiosity had done fine work for me again, turning my long, loose curls to a deep red almost the same hue as my dress.

There the elegance ended, for it had quickly occurred to me that I couldn't leave the puppy alone. I'd thought briefly of taking her back to Miranda, Boss of Beasts, for the morning's activities, and collecting her again when I got back. But I abandoned that idea almost as quickly as it came up, because the puppy was unlikely to consent. It did

3

not matter what Miranda did to keep the puppy under her eye; she would always escape, by means largely unknown, and find her way back to me. If I left her with Miranda, she'd escape again and come looking — but she would find no trace of me. Would she be upset? I could not take that risk, for she had been starving to death when I'd found her and that was only a few days ago. She was frail, and in need of constant care. I wasn't leaving her behind.

The fact that I had entirely lost my heart to the little beast was neither here nor there, of course. But who could help it? She was completely adorable. She had the kind of silky fur that begged to be touched, and it was bright gold. Perky little ears, enormous nose, tiny unicorn horn — what's not to love about all that? She was affectionate, too, and she made me feel needed.

If that makes for a rather pathetic vision of me, I can only apologise.

Anyway, having decided to take her along, I was then obliged to add an inelegantly enormous bag to my attire. It had to be big enough to hold a significant supply of milk for the puppy, for she had to be fed once an hour and I had no idea how long the Baron intended to monopolise my company. She got cold easily, too, even in the balmy weather, so I stashed blankets and fluffies galore to wrap her up in at need. Then I made a nest in the top for the puppy, installed her therein, and tramped down to the hall, already annoyed by the heavy, unwieldy bag by the time I had made it down a mere two of the House's many winding flights of stairs.

C'est la vie.

There was no sign of the Baron, but when I peeped out of the grand front door I saw him at once. Being Baron Alban, he simply cannot do anything in either a conventional way or a low-key way. Why wear a typical suit, however well-cut, when you can appear in a splendid top hat and a nineteenth-century frock coat? Or a nice set of nineteen-thirties tweeds, as was the case today, and he had the car to match. Don't ask me what kind of car it was, for I haven't the first clue, but it had the swanky, exaggerated curves of a proper old-time automobile, and it gleamed in gorgeous British Racing Green. Alban sat at the wheel, wearing tan leather driving gloves and a dark fedora. He grinned as I trotted out into the driveway, and tipped his hat to me.

He then proceeded to get out and hold the passenger door for me, which made me feel quite the lady — at least until the shoulder-bag I had lumbered myself with swung around as I was getting in, knocking me off-balance, and I all but fell into the seat. My poor dignity.

I hastily checked to make sure the puppy was unharmed, and found her to be fast asleep.

Alban returned to the driver's seat, and I took the opportunity to stash the bag safely by my feet, propped securely upright so the puppy would not fall out.

'I know the best place for breakfast,' he informed me as he turned the car, and my stomach was very happy to hear it.

We drove for about twenty minutes, and I began to suspect some kind of shenanigans. Now, I am notorious at Home for being spectacularly poor at finding my way around, and it is partly because I struggle to recognise places I have already been to, if it is nowhere especially familiar to me. So at first I was not troubled by the fact that the roads we were hurtling down rung no bells whatsoever with me; was I likely to remember this particular country road, hedge-lined and flanked by fields, over another almost exactly like it? No.

But after a while, there began to be a change. The hawthorn, blackthorn and hazel hedges ceased to look quite so much like hawthorn, blackthorn or hazel and developed a different appearance altogether. They were taller, for one, and thicker, their leaves a brighter green and oddly curly. Some of them were dotted with star-like flowers of unusual size. The roads that ran in between lost their tarmac-look and became a smooth stone, pale and apparently indestructible, considering the total lack of holes (and believe me, back country roads with no holes in are pretty rare). When a bird flew overhead that in no way resembled an English bird, but more nearly reminded me of a hare with wings, I was certain. 'Just where exactly are we?' I asked.

'The Troll Roads,' answered the Baron serenely.

'And they are?'

'Hidden ways across the world. It's a tradition dating back hundreds of years, though these days the standard of the roads is a bit higher. They had to be upgraded when cars happened.'

I could see there were a few advantages to these Roads, one of them being a total lack of other traffic. This particular one also had the look of a place where it literally never rains. Quite possibly it did not.

'We're going to my home Enclave,' offered the Baron, when I said no more. 'Rhaditton.'

Rhaditton. The word had the old-fashioned air of a top boarding school, and considering that the Baron was attached to the Troll Court, I could well believe it was a salubrious place, and probably exclusive. 'I did not know you lived so close to us at the Society,' I said.

He grinned at me. 'I don't. That is why we're taking the Troll Roads.'

I blinked. 'They're faster?'

'Much.'

'How?'

'Because they're magick.'

Of course.

He laughed, inferring from my silence — rightly enough — that I found this answer inadequate. 'Waymasters,' he said, more helpfully. 'Quite a number of them have worked on the Roads over the years. The routes aren't as good as a Waymaster in person, of course, but they're not a bad alternative.'

'So what do they do, sort of... swoosh you along?'

'Something like that, yes. Waymasters used to be adept at a range of travel arts, once upon a time. One or two of them still are.'

Jay had said something like that, recently — that Way-mastery was a diminished art these days, with magick on the decline. Jay, of course, was still quite able to spirit himself and others from henge to henge in a single step, across vast distances, so his "diminished" arts still looked pretty impressive to me.

Ten minutes later, we rolled up outside the vast, gleaming walls of a city. Seriously, it looked like Minas Tirith or something, all white stone and shining in the sun like a slice of heaven on earth. The gates opened as the Baron's car approached, literally like magick, and in we went.

Aaaand I have never been anywhere so glorious in my life. Eerily glorious, because to go with all the polished stone buildings, intricately carved walls, gilding — yes, actual *gilding* — and general air of improbable luxury, there were none of the things one might normally expect to see in a city that's lived in by real people. Litter here and there, for example. Peeling paint, shabby old houses in need of maintenance, an occasional abandoned bicycle or shopping trolley.

I was left wondering how far people like Baron Alban qualified as *real*. Everything about him was improbably fabulous, including his choice of abode.

I tried not to gawk too obviously as we rolled through street after street of this opulence, and in all likelihood failed. At last we drew up outside a low, greyish stone place with an ornate roof and an array of elegant chairs and tables arranged outside. I don't think they were solid gold, but it was hard to tell.

'Ah, of course,' I said as the car drew to a stop. 'This is how you do cafes in Rhaditton.'

'They do fantastic pancakes,' said the Baron.

Pancakes seemed mundane under the circumstances, but I was soon reassured on this point. A few minutes later, I was seated inside the building in what was probably the best seat in the place, with a fine view out of the grand window all the way down the wide boulevard beyond. Baron Alban sat at my elbow; the bag with the puppy in was set on the seat beside me; and I had a plate of pancakes before me that would make any reasonable person cry with happiness.

Point one: they were troll-sized helpings, approximately the size of dinner plates, and there were a lot of them.

Point two: they were smothered in everything. Everything, everything. Ice cream, fruits in improbable colours that I'd never seen before, some kind of sticky sauce that glistened so invitingly it could only be (as the Baron would put it) magick.

I took a spoonful of all this glory, and almost died.

As I was busy winging my way to heaven upon a tide of sweet delight, Baron Alban sat sipping a tall cup of something steamy, his own plate virtually untouched. He was watching me, with a smile that said, *you are inelegantly devoted to food, but I like it.*

I was unmoved. Nothing was getting in between me and those pancakes, not even the desire to appear cool before the fabulousness that was the Baron.

'What's the bag for?' he said after a while.

Having by that time devoured enough to quieten the complaints of my half-starved stomach, I found myself at leisure to answer him. 'I'll tell you later.'

All right, *briefly* to answer him.

He grinned. 'Fair.'

'If you aren't going to eat,' I said, eyeing his plate with disfavour, 'then you can talk. What's the hurry today?'

'The hurry?' he smiled at me, far too innocently for my liking. 'Just wanted to finally get some time with you.'

'At seven in the morning? I do not buy it, Mister.'

'Actually, "my lord Baron" would be more appropriate,' he said, his grin widening.

'Diversion failed, my lord Baron. What are we doing here?'

'Is it so hard to believe I might merely want your company?'

Thinking of the salubrious city and its equally glamorous residents — I'd seen several gorgeous and gorgeously dressed troll ladies wandering those streets, and an example sat not six feet away at another table — I said, 'Yes.'

To my mild regret, the Baron began to look sheepish. I suppose a small part of me *had* hoped he was just desperate for my company.

Such is life.

He picked up his fork and took a bite of pancake, clearly a delaying tactic.

'Spit it out,' I recommended. 'Not the pancake! The problem.'

'I didn't want you to think I'd invited you just to—'

'I know, I know,' I said. I thought it best to interrupt before things could get any more awkward. 'You were positively dying to see me, and it *also* happens that there's something on your mind?'

He smiled at me, with that twinkle in his bright green eyes that makes it impossible to be annoyed with him. 'Exactly.'

'Always nice to kill two birds with one stone.'

'I always thought that expression unnecessarily blood-thirsty.'

'It is. So the problem is what?'

'Right.' He pushed aside his plate, quite flabbergasting me, and folded his arms upon the table-top. 'I heard a rumour,' he began.

2

'JUST THE ONE RUMOUR?' I said. 'Remarkable.'

The Baron's irresistible smile flashed. 'Actually, more than one.'

'Let's have the first one, then.'

'Is it true that there's a leak inside the Society?'

That was unexpected. I filled my mouth with ice cream and fruit, stalling for a few moments to think. What should I tell him?

He wasn't wrong. Things had got pretty interesting at work lately. We'd discovered an incredibly rare and indescribably valuable artefact (a book, talkative); faced off against a new, but nonetheless powerful rival organisation with the downright fatuous name of Ancestria Magicka who were determined to steal it; and almost got eaten alive by a haunted house and its trio of unfriendly ghosts. In the middle of all this, we'd found that word of the chatty book (Bill) had somehow leaked out, despite the fact that it had never left Home. That's how we ended up with Ancestria Magicka on our tails.

Furthermore, it wasn't just information that had gone farther than it should. Someone had actively sabotaged us by putting tracker spells on the book itself. It was clear that somebody at the Society was a turncoat, and that was alarming. But how had the Baron found out?

'Who told you that?' I finally said. 'I wasn't aware that Milady was disposed to chat about it.'

'Someone high up in the Society contacted the Troll Court a few days ago with word of a problem,' answered the Baron. 'Probably Milady herself, in fact. She requested aid.'

'Did they send you to nose around?'

He smiled, sheepish again. 'Might have.'

Hmm. It was plausible enough that Milady might seek aid from the Court. I'd become aware of more than one link between Milady, whoever she was behind the vague title, and the Troll Courts of old; if she could no longer be sure of who to trust at Home, it was not so far-fetched that she would consult her allies.

She had not mentioned it to me, though. Did that mean I, too, was suspect? I didn't think so, but I still felt a slight twinge.

I gave the Baron a brief precis of everything that had happened with the book, which he heard without interruption. 'At present we have no idea who it might be,' I said in conclusion. 'Bill caused a sensation at Home, as you might imagine. For a little while, everybody found some excuse to pass through the Library and gawk at the book. Any of them could have passed information to Ancestria, and far too many had at least some opportunity to plant a tracker spell on it. We know that someone's rotten, but we have no leads whatsoever.'

The Baron took a forkful, and chewed meditatively, his eyes faraway. 'There is a reason Milady contacted the Court,' he finally said. 'There are some ancient magicks that are only really practiced by a rare few nowadays, and the Court makes a habit of collecting them up. Sort of the way you do — preservation tactic. If we don't find and nurture those talents, the magicks might fade away altogether.'

'Quite,' I murmured.

'There used to be something called a Truthseeker, or so it was known until about the middle of the nineteenth century, by which time there were so few of them left that the word itself fell out of use. There are no human Truthseekers anymore, but there is one living who can still employ that art, and he's at the Court.'

This sounded promising. 'And Truthseeking consists of what?'

'A Truthseeker is unusually sensitive to...' He took a mouthful of his drink, and shrugged. 'I don't pretend to know how it works, Ves, you'll have to ask him. But where you and I can only guess at whether or not we're being told the truth, a Truthseeker has a much more solid idea. What's more, they can, to some degree, compel a person to speak the truth. Milady means to question the Society about the Bill incident, and she's requested our Truthseeker's presence at those interviews.'

'Fair enough. But what's your role in all this?'

'I'm the advance party. Seeing as I already have a contact at the Society, and a pretty spectacular one at that—' He paused here to waggle his eyebrows at me, which was far more charming than it had any right to be —'I was sent to get the details straight from the source.'

'Well, you've got the details.' I smiled at him, hoping my lips were not as visibly sugar-crusted as I feared. 'I doubt I've told you anything more than Milady already relayed, though.'

'It's good to get a fuller account.' He was being generous, but he was good at doing it unobtrusively, so I overlooked it. 'The other thing...' he said, and hesitated again.

'Oh yes, rumour number two. Let's hear it.'

'You found something...unusual, recently?'

'My dear Baron, we are the Society for Magickal Heritage and I am one of its finest field agents. Our entire job consists of going out into the world and finding highly interesting things whose existence is probably under threat. Could you be more specific?'

That sheepish smile again. 'Of course. Uh, the existence of this particular thing is not so much under threat as... disputed? Extinguished? Impossible?'

'Oh! You mean the puppy.'

He blinked at me. 'It's a puppy?'

'Not in the way you are thinking. Miranda called it a dappledok pup. No relation to the canine species of creature, I'm fairly sure. I may someday get very, very tired of asking you this, but: how did you hear about that?'

'Milady again, but she was cagey about it. Dropped a hint, primarily by asking if we happened to have any experts on extinct magickal beasts mooching around at the Court.'

'Do you?'

'Yes, but she's somewhere in the Caribbean right now, on the trail of some impossibly rare bird whose name I have forgotten.'

'Were you sent to ask me about the pup, too, or is this mere private curiosity?'

'Some of both.' His eyes strayed to the bag I had left leaning innocently against the back of the adjacent chair.

Too sharp for his own good, that Baron.

'All right, all right,' I said, rolling my eyes at him. 'I'll show you.' I lifted the bag's flap, carefully in case the puppy fell out. But she was still tucked securely in the nest I had made out of three pairs of socks, and still asleep. She was so motionless that for a moment my heart stopped, but when I touched her, I could feel the slow rise and fall of her furred side. I tickled her.

She did not move.

'She sleeps like a champion,' I said to the Baron. 'She has had a hard time of it, though. Her siblings starved, and she wasn't far off going the same way when we found her.'

'Let her sleep, then,' said the Baron, staring at her with his eyes as wide as saucers and a dopey grin on his face.

It wasn't just me who found her utterly charming, then. Reassuring.

She was looking particularly cute, all curled up in a tiny ball barely larger than an orange. She has tufts of goldish hair growing around the base of her little unicorn horn, the tips of which swayed with the rhythm of her breathing.

'I imagine she will wake up soon, for it's time for her feed, and she's not one to miss out on breakfast.' Neither am I, of course, though I have nothing like her excuse. Nobody's ever tried to starve *me*. Nonetheless, I felt that it made us kindred spirits.

I noticed Baron Alban eyeing my cleared plate, probably thinking along similar lines. He refrained, however, from comment.

Wise man.

It probably was more than an hour since she had last had her milk, so I opted to tickle her until she woke. She did so at last with a grumpy little snort, and sat up, stretching. I was ready with her bottle, and she soon clamped her jaws around the teat and got to work.

The Baron and I watched with the breathless silence of brand new, doting parents.

'You know what a dappledok pup is, of course?' said the Baron after a while.

'Other than the fact that it's been completely extinct since the eighteenth century?'

'It has indeed. But before that?'

'No. I asked Miranda but she gabbled something largely incoherent — she was wrestling with a clawed, very un-happy creature at the time, in her defence — and I never did make sense of it.' I'd asked Val, too. Her response had been, "I'll get back to you," which meant that she did not know at that precise moment where the books were on that topic, but she would soon find out.

'Spriggans,' said Alban, incomprehensibly.

'I beg your pardon?'

'Fae-folk, native to Cornwall. Fond of shiny stuff. They bred the dappledoks out of a few other fae beasts, the goal being to create a species with a nose for treasure. They were said to be amazing trackers of anything or anyone carrying gold.'

I was quiet, because only the previous day I had gone into my jewellery drawer for my favourite gold ear-studs and found them missing. I'd assumed I had simply put them somewhere they shouldn't be, but suddenly I wondered.

'How did they come to die out?' I asked.

His mouth twisted in a grimace. 'Think it through, Ves. Cute, largely defenceless little creatures that are literally the road to riches? Spriggans can be unwisely boastful, to boot. Word spread, everyone wanted a dappledok, and... the rate of thefts across Britain, the Enclaves, the Dells, everywhere, positively soared. In the end they were banned. It became illegal to breed them. They survived a while after that, of course, through secret breeding-programmes, but eventually they petered out.'

'Spriggans,' I said.

'Spriggans.'

This was not the very best of news, for the fae-folk can be tricky. To say the least. There are more of them still about than non-magickers tend to think; they've just learned to hide better than they used to. But they can still

20

cause a world of trouble for magickers and non-magickers alike, and spriggans... well, they have a reputation for being among the worst for sheer hell-raising mischief.

I've tried to avoid tangling with the fae as much as possible.

'So did I tell you where I found this pup?' I said.

'Pray do.'

Remember when I said we'd almost been swallowed by a haunted house? That's where we found the pup: curled up in a corner with two others, both dead. And this particular house was the kind that moves around, courtesy of its resident ghost of a Waymaster. It dated from the fourteen hundreds, if not even earlier, and it really felt like it.

I told all this to the Baron.

'Triple haunting?' he mused. 'That's unusual.'

'Yes. But. While I did not have much opportunity to chat with the residents, it did not strike me as likely that any of them would have cared much about operating a secret dappledok breeding programme. What would be the point?'

'So you think someone else might have been using the cottage?'

'Presumably with their consent, yes. It's possible. Or someone merely dumped the pups there. Or the pups might even have found their own way in.'

'In other words, you have no idea.'

'None whatsoever.'

The Baron's green, green eyes laughed at me again. 'Excellent,' he said. 'Good talk.'

I grinned back. 'I might be able to find something out,' I offered.

'Do you know, I was hoping you might say that?'

3

LATER, HAPPILY REPLETE WITH pancakes and with the Baron's teasing smile echoing in my mind, I wandered through the corridors at Home with my shoulder bag clutched to my chest, whispering soothing words to the pup. She wanted to get out, but Alban's words made me wary. She was more valuable even than I had imagined; not just supposedly extinct, but a potential source of riches. And if we indeed had a mole wandering these same hallways, it suddenly seemed like a very poor idea to show her off.

I was heading for the east wing, and Miranda's quarters in the Magickal Beasts division. I needed to talk to her right away.

Unusually, she was not to be found among any of her creatures. I trawled through room after room, eyed a seemingly endless succession of cages, pens and indoor pad-docks, and though a dazzling array of weird and wonderful creatures met my eyes, there was no Miranda.

I found her at last in the east wing common room, apparently meditating over a cup of coffee, and firmly ensconced in a deep, plumply-stuffed arm chair. At least, she did not look up when I walked in, her gaze remaining fixed upon the window. I looked. There was nothing much going on outside, though the view was quite lovely: sunlight glinted on the meadows surrounding the House, and given the time of year the grasses were all frilly and much strewn with new flowers.

Serene and gorgeous as it was, I didn't think it likely that Miranda was quite so mesmerised by it as all that.

'Mir?' I said, when she still did not appear to notice my presence.

Her head turned, and she blinked at me. 'Yes! Sorry, I was miles away.'

'I noticed. Everything all right?'

'Yep,' she said succinctly, and smiled. Never one for long speeches, Miranda.

I offered her the bag, which she took, setting her coffee cup down on a side table. 'Nice puppy nest,' she commented, opening the flap.

'I've been hearing all about dappledoks today, and the news isn't all good,' I told her. 'You probably know what they were once used for?'

Miranda gave me a quizzical look. 'Used for? There was an odd reference in one letter to "treasure-dogs" and something similar in a book I once browsed through, but it was an offhand comment. Their gold fur is probably enough to account for such notions, and perhaps those horns — they're being conflated with legendary creatures. Superstition more than anything.'

'Perhaps not.' I related the Baron's tale, which prompted a frown from Miranda.

'Banned by who?' she said, once I had finished. 'The Troll Court?'

'That was the implication, though if it succeeded in wiping out the dappledoks I conclude it must have been agreed upon, and enforced by, most of the magickal councils of the day.'

'Which would be highly unusual.'

'Wouldn't it? I got to thinking. A spate of thefts would be unwelcome and disruptive, to be sure, but if the response was such a total and inflexible ban, then I wonder what it was that the pups were digging up?'

'Did you ask his Baronship?'

I had, of course, prior to our leaving the improbably wonderful café. But predictably enough, he had merely twinkled at me and fended off my questions with distractions, charm, counter-questions or, when I proved impervious to any of that, the flat statement of: 'Court secrets, Ves. Sorry.'

He ought to have known better than to say that to me.

'Stonewalled me,' I told Miranda.

'Scandal,' she said with a grin. 'Intriguing.'

'So, I am going to do some digging. In the meantime, the pup is a problem. If there is anybody else floating around who knows that the Legend of Dappledok might have some truth to it, I don't want them finding out that we happen to have one. Do we have anybody good enough at illusion to camouflage a living creature?'

'Oh, several. Leave her with me, and I'll get somebody to come up here and sort her out.'

'If she looks like a chihuahua or a dachshund or something, nobody would question that.'

Miranda shook her head. 'Too mundane. This is the Society, and you're Cordelia Vesper — flamboyant to a fault, and notorious for being up to your elbows in magick all the livelong day. We'll make her look like a miniature gorhound or something.'

'Purple,' I said.

Miranda raised her brows.

'This thing?' I said, raising my left hand to show her the Curiosity I always wear: the ring that changes the colour of my hair. 'It works on animals, too.'

'Hah. Purple it is.'

I DISLIKED WALKING OUT of there without my pup with me, but it was in a good cause. Anyway, there is no one at the Society who can be better relied upon to take good care of her than Miranda.

I was on my way to Val, next, but my phone buzzed. When I grabbed it, there was no call to answer or message to read: instead, the lock screen displayed an animated image of a handsome, eighteenth-century chocolate pot of wrought silver, glittering steam coiling from its spout.

Or in other words, Milady wanted to see me.

I changed course at once, and headed for the stairs.

Once I had finished laboriously climbing up to the very top of the tallest tower, I discovered that the summons had not been limited to just me. Waymaster Jay was already there, and — more interestingly — Val. Valerie, Queen of the Library, is rarely dragged all the way up to Milady's tower. It might be because it is somewhat harder for her to get up there than the rest of us, seeing as she's confined to her chair (albeit a witched-up, conveniently floating one). But the House has a helpful way of whisking her anywhere she wants to go in the blink of an eye, so it's more likely that Val simply has the kind of autonomy at Home that the rest of us can only dream of.

I was the last to arrive, apparently, for the tower door closed behind me, and the incorporeal voice of Milady began at once to speak.

'Chairs, please, dear,' she said.

It took me a moment to realise that she had not, in fact, addressed any of the three of us by that unusually endearing title, but had been speaking to the House. Chairs promptly appeared for Jay and me: nice, fatly stuffed ones in tapestry upholstery, very comfy indeed.

This worried me. Milady rarely provided chairs. How long did she expect us to be here for?

I took a chair anyway, sinking gratefully into its plush embrace. I may be well used to the long climb to the top of the House, but I don't care how fit you are, it is still tiring.

Jay smiled at me. 'Had fun?'

Word really travels fast at the Society.

'Yes,' I said. 'There were pancakes.'

'An incomparable date.'

Well, sort of. I was still stinging just a bit from the fact that the Baron's purpose had been so very all business, but

I did not feel like admitting that to Jay. Call it pride, if you will. So I said, 'Completely,' and let the subject drop, for Milady interposed.

'Good morning,' she said. 'Thank you all for coming. As you are unhappily aware, we have had a... situation at Home, which has not yet been resolved. And since we are on the brink of another, I consider it wise to discuss our options.'

'Another?' I said, startled.

'Relating to your recent find at the cottage, Ves.'

'We do seem to have a talent for making spectacular, but highly inconvenient finds,' murmured Jay.

'You certainly do,' I said. 'First Bill, then the pup. I wait with breathless anticipation to see what you'll stumble over next.'

Jay flashed me a smug smile.

'And whether or not we will survive it.'

The smile disappeared.

Milady cleared her throat. 'First of all, let me assure you that I do not anticipate a repeat of the Bill incident. While clearly special, a dappledok pup is in no way likely to be as fiercely sought-after as a book like that — or its creator. Nor are its unusual talents widely known about, or much believed in nowadays.'

'Really?' I said. 'The pup is basically a gold mine.'

'Not so much,' said Jay. 'It's not fifteen thirty-seven anymore. People don't store their wealth as stacks of gold or jewels anymore. When they do have valuables, they're in safes — or behind stoutly locked doors protected by house alarms. I wouldn't say a dappledok is useless in two thousand seventeen, but the best she could do is facilitate a few petty thefts.'

'Fair enough,' I had to agree. 'But you're talking about the non-magicker world. What about *our* world? We know little about her talents. Is it just gold and silver she can sniff out? Jewels? What jewels? Imagine if she could stick her little nose to the ground and trundle off after, say, a major Wand or something.'

'And that is a fair point, Ves,' said Milady. 'So I am pleased to hear that you have taken steps to have the pup disguised. It is a reasonable precaution, at least until we are able to discover the extent of the pup's talents.'

'What's the nature of the situation, then?' asked Jay.

'As Ves will already be aware, I have sought help with the matter of the... disloyalty we have sadly suffered among our ranks. I would first like to privately assure you all that I do not in the smallest degree doubt your integrity. I will, however, ask that you submit to an interview with the Truthseeker, like the rest of your peers.'

'A Truthseeker?' Jay whistled. 'I didn't know there were any of those left.'

'There are not many. Regarding the other matter, has it occurred to you to wonder in any detail where the pup came from?'

'Somewhat,' I said. 'I do not think the cottage had much to do with it. For the breed to survive for two centuries, there must have been a concerted effort going on somewhere to preserve it. But if it has remained a secret all this time, then it must be somewhere very, very hidden. How those three pups came to be in the cottage I couldn't say, but it certainly wasn't equipped for a breeding programme on that scale, and it showed no signs of having been inhabited by anybody living for a long time. The source must lie elsewhere.'

'They are also delicate,' Val added. 'Difficult to breed, almost as difficult to nurse to adulthood. It would take specialist knowledge, and a great deal of time and money to bring it off.'

'Which suggests,' I said, 'that somebody out there has a clear purpose in mind for them.'

'Might have been using them for something all along,' said Jay.

Good point. Electrifying point. I sat up, my thoughts awhirl.

'Exactly,' said Milady. 'And that is the situation. I need you to find out more about the dappledoks. Find out what they can really do, and discover where this one came from.

It is still illegal to breed dappledok pups; Valerie has gone to significant trouble to verify this. That means that there is a group out there, or even a whole organisation, who have devoted considerable effort to an illegal breeding operation and they will not have done this lightly. It must be put a stop to.'

Thorny issue. On the one hand, protecting magickal beasts was a big part of our job; we were supposed to *prevent* them from dying out, not uphold a law that basically compelled them to do so. But I could not fault Milady's thinking. These pups were something else. There must have been a solid reason for their banning in the first place; that reason, whatever it was, might well be as true now as it was centuries ago.

I tried not to dwell on the fact that our having a dappledok on the premises at all was effectively a crime. What would become of the poor little pup? She was an innocent in the business. It was not her fault that her huge, gawky nose was all kinds of magickal.

That would be a problem for later.

4

'Yes,' added Milady. 'You may wish to begin by consulting your book.'

'Bill Two? By all means. He probably knows something about dappledoks.'

'Ask him about the Spriggan Dells, too,' Milady suggested. 'Not just the ones in Cornwall. Spriggans spread much beyond the borders of that county some time ago, and it may be no accident that this pup turned up in East Anglia.'

Then again, it might. The cottage did, after all, have a habit of moving around a lot.

Val spoke up. 'Something else you can ask Bill, Ves. Quite a lot of major artefacts have gone missing down the ages. Some of them have turned up again, some haven't yet. I would be interested to hear what Bill knows about that, considering he's spent time at the Library of Farringale.' She frowned. 'Or, his predecessor did. Does Bill Two have all the same information?'

'Yes,' said Jay. 'Indira made an exact duplicate.'

Valerie's eyes gleamed in a way I did not quite like. 'Can I borrow that book, Ves?'

'Are you planning to give it back?'

She thought about that. 'Would "someday" do?'

'Not really.'

'Books belong in the Library!' Val protested.

'But this one's mine!'

Valerie folded her arms, and stared implacably at the spot in mid-air where Milady's voice somehow manifested sparkles. 'Can I request a second duplicate for the Library?' she said.

'Yes,' said Milady.

Valerie brightened at once. 'I'll talk to Indira.'

'Orlando,' corrected Milady. 'Indira is assisting on this project.'

'Nobody talks to Orlando,' said Valerie, rolling her eyes. 'You mean *send a requisition form up to the attic and hope he notices.*'

'He will notice. Valerie, please continue to consult the Library's existing resources, and relay anything you find to Ves and Jay.'

'Of course, Milady.'

'Jay, I imagine a visit to the site where you found the pup may shortly be in order. If you will be so kind as to facilitate the journey?'

'Certainly.'

'The Spriggan Glades are a different matter. They will have to be consulted, but I do not recommend that you do so immediately. They can be prickly, and difficult to deal with. I am endeavouring to secure a guide for you.'

I wondered if this guide might prove to be, in fact, a spriggan. Could be. Fae folk rarely mixed much with the human worlds, trolls somewhat excepted. They kept to themselves, tucked away in their own Dells, Glades, Knowes and whatever else, and did not much set foot outside. But still, it was not unheard of for a fae to enrol at the Hidden University, and the Society had even had a few on their staff at one point or another. I wouldn't be in the least surprised if Milady's guide turned out to be... unusual.

We stayed a while longer, bouncing thoughts around about the pup and its possible origins. Since it was nothing but speculation, Milady called a halt eventually and sent us off. 'Keep me informed,' she said as we trailed out of the tower.

I made her my usual curtsey on the way out. What can I say, Milady inspires a few old-fashioned impulses. 'Yes, ma'am,' I said.

35

The air sparkled. 'There's chocolate in the pots.'

POTS, PLURAL. THERE WAS one waiting in my room, and two cups: for Jay and for me. Valerie sent me a snapshot of the second one adorning her desk in the Library: it was gold, and it had purple smoke coming out of the spout.

'Huh,' grunted Jay, eyeing our much more mundane-looking silver one with some suspicion.

'Valerie and Milady go way back,' I told him, contentedly pouring hot chocolate into the two cups. The chocolate itself was too amazing to care very much about the vessel.

'And you two don't? How long have you worked here?'

'Only about a decade.'

He blinked. 'Only? How long's Val been here?'

'Since forever, as far as I can tell.'

'Not, like, literally.'

I grinned, enjoying the stupefied look on his face. 'Probably not literally, but who knows? We are all about secrets at the Society.'

Jay shook his head. 'Bill Two,' he prompted me, accepting his cup from me with a smile of anticipation.

'Right.' I found the strength of will to set my cup down after only a single sip of the deliciously rich contents, and retrieved the Book.

I have a safe in my snug little room. I call it a safe more for convenience than because it represents the arrangement with any particular accuracy. It is actually a… well, it is a chamber pot. Don't judge me. What could be more perfect? It is not even an attractive chamber pot, merely the plain white porcelain kind. It even has a crack in it.

See, if you barge into my room looking for valuables, the last place you bother poking your nose into is the ancient, cobweb-wreathed chamber pot lying under the bed, right in the back corner. If you did, all you would see is a dead spider.

Enchantments can be such fun.

Jay made no comment when I fell to my knees and began rooting under the bed, but one eyebrow rose when I emerged with the chamber pot. 'Did Bill Two urgently need to relieve himself?'

'He is a book, Jay. He is above such things.'

Jay's other eyebrow went up. 'Does he *sleep* in a chamber pot?'

I did something fancy with my hands. It was not at all necessary, of course, but it looks impressive. Without it, the process of magick looks sadly underwhelming.

When I had finished waving my hands about, the chamber pot more nearly resembled a rainbow crystal chest with an enormous lock on the front. Into this I inserted a matching crystal key, and the lid sprung open.

Jay put his face in his hands. 'It's rainbow,' he muttered, muffled.

'Of course it is.' I lifted Bill Two out, left the chest on the bed, and returned to my chair — and my cup of chocolate. 'Right. Hi, Bill Two.' I settled the book in my lap, and took a moment to admire it yet again. It is the big, heavy, ancient-looking kind, with purple leather covers and a twelve-pointed star on the front. Devastatingly handsome.

'Might I be so forward as to request an alternative name?' said the book. 'It is lowering to be addressed by my predecessor's appellation.'

'Of course! I ought to have thought of it before now. Did you have any particular name in mind?'

'Well,' said the book, sounding suddenly diffident. 'I have always rather liked the word "gallimaufry."'

The book that knows everything *would* have a spectacular vocabulary, wouldn't it? 'A wonderful name,' I said.

Jay leaned in my direction. 'What does that mean?' he whispered.

'It means an assortment of different kinds of things.'

'Fitting.'

'Entirely. Gallimaufry it shall be!'

The book riffled its pages contentedly.

'Shall you object very much to being addressed as Galli?' I hazarded. 'Gallimaufry is a lengthy word for regular use.'

'Why not Mauf?' said Jay.

I glared at him. 'Let's not confuse the issue—'

'I find Mauf agreeable,' said the book.

'Um. In that case, Mauf it is.'

Jay smiled.

I took a gulp of chocolate. 'Mauf,' I began. 'We are here to consult you on a matter of some importance.'

The book brightened, and I do mean that literally. The twelve-pointed star embossed into the surface gleamed with silver fire, and the dark purple of the leather lightened a few shades. 'I shall be delighted to help!' Mauf declared.

He liked to feel important. I had already noticed that. 'We rely on you,' I added, laying it on a bit.

Mauf preened. 'How may I assist you?'

'There is a situation at the Society regarding the sudden re-emergence of the dappledok species,' I began.

'Which dappledok species?' said Mauf.

I exchanged a startled look with Jay. 'Which?' I repeated. 'What do you mean?'

'Dappledok is a Dell situated near the south coast of Cornwall,' Mauf informed us. 'Once famed for their talent with beasts of all kinds, its residents engaged in a number of selective breeding programmes and produced an array of hitherto unknown creatures with unusual, and highly desirable, abilities.'

'What?' I gulped chocolate, my head spinning. 'There are *more*?'

'I know of at least eight.'

I looked at Jay, eyes wide. He stared back.

'Um,' I said. 'I don't think Miranda knows anything about that.'

'I don't think Milady even knows,' said Jay. 'Or Valerie either.'

'Right. Bill — Mauf — we are referring to a dog-like creature with golden fur and a single horn between its ears.'

'The Nose-for-Gold, that being the literal translation of the original name in the spriggan tongue. Or Goldnose, as they were informally known in English.'

'That sounds about right.'

'Last referenced somewhere in the seventeen hundreds,' said Mauf. 'Believed to have become extinct sometime thereafter.'

'That agrees with what Miranda told me. It's true that they can sniff out valuable objects?'

'It is, but the use of said power was banned by the Troll Court in 1703, the Magickal Councils of the Dells and Dales in 1704, and most of the various fae monarchs by 1706. This did not, of course, deter very many, and so the breeding of the Goldnoses themselves was subsequently forbidden.'

'Even the fae monarchs banned them?' I said, surprised. 'But were they not created by spriggans?'

'The spriggan queen, Parlewin, was the first to declare them outlawed. It is recorded that her favourite brooch, a gaudy object made from gold and rainbow diamonds, vanished under mysterious circumstances in early 1705 and since her primary rival at court was known to be in possession of a trio of Goldnoses, the culprit seemed, to her majesty, obvious enough.'

Jay grinned. 'Perhaps it did not occur to the original breeders that anyone might be audacious enough to use it on *them.*'

'Mauf,' I said. 'Do you know of anyone who defied the ban?'

'It is written that many did, at first, and the penalties for flouting the law had to be significantly increased. This proved effective, and over the next fifty years or so recorded instances of Goldnoses being bred gradually dwindled to nothing.'

'What penalty did they impose?' asked Jay.

'The worst penalty ever suffered for illegal ownership of a Goldnose was Divesting.'

'Um,' I said as my stomach fell through the floor. 'Is... is that still valid?'

'In some communities, yes,' said Mauf.

'Argh,' I said.

See, Divesting is a nice euphemism for the total stripping of all of a person's magickal abilities. Forever. I do not even know how it is done; few do. Only the highest authorities in the land are capable of it, and it is usually handed out only in cases of extreme misuse of magick.

Was I in danger of *that*, for rescuing a puppy?!

'Do not trouble yourself unduly,' said Mauf kindly. 'This law applies in those magickal communities or countries which date back to the early eighteenth century, namely the Troll Court, the faerie courts, the Magickal Councils of the Dells and Dales, the—'

'But *not* the Hidden Ministry?' I interjected, unable to bear the suspense while Mauf rattled through another forty-three or so such organisations.

'Indeed not. The Ministry was founded in 1787, by which time the problem of the Goldnoses had so far receded into the past that it was not thought necessary to carry over that particular law. As such, Ves, you are presently committing no official crime.'

He did not need to add that this would only hold true until somebody thought it worth their while to write up a new law about it. I decided not to think about that because something more immediately pressing occurred to me. 'But I was when I took the pup into Rhaditton!'

'Arguably only. There is no actual prohibition against having a Goldnose pup with you in Troll territory, provided you are neither engaged in using it nor in breeding more.'

Phew. 'Thank you, Mauf,' I said.

Jay patted my shoulder comfortingly, which I took to mean that my brief panic had been showing on my face. Don't get me wrong, I will cheerfully bend any number of rules when I feel it is necessary. But outright flouting inscribed magickal law is another matter, and this is not exactly an emergency situation going on here. No one wants to risk a Divesting without thoroughly good reason.

I'd lost my train of thought by then, and could not immediately think of what next to enquire of Mauf. Luckily Jay still had his wits about him. 'Mauf, can you think of anybody who might have managed to maintain the Goldnose breed since the eighteenth century into the present, and without detection?'

'Until now,' I amended.

Mauf fell silent for a while. Was he thinking? Could a book like him (or more rightly, it) think, in the real sense of the word? Was he riffling through all his archives? I wondered, not for the first time, how so powerful yet peculiar an enchantment worked.

'Not immediately,' said Mauf at last. 'There are no recorded instances of any concerted breeding programmes

43

in operation since 1727, when a group of renegade sprig-gans were found to have established a miniature state for themselves in an otherwise abandoned Dell. They were all imprisoned, and it is not written that they ever escaped, or that they were ever released.'

I sighed, a little bit disappointed. But I suppose life would be far too easy if Mauf had an easy answer to every-thing. Wouldn't it? Challenges are good for the character, right?

Right.

5

'LET'S THINK,' SAID JAY. 'Hidden Ministry aside, the Goldnoses are still banned in virtually every magickal community there is. It is no mean feat, then, to breed them in spite of the law, and to keep it going for so long. It also takes considerable courage to consistently flout a law which carries such severe penalties for disobedience. Somebody really, really wanted those pups.'

'Takes courage, or confidence?' I suggested. 'You might flout that law with impunity if you felt that you had the right people on your side.'

Jay blinked at me. 'You mean somebody high in authority might be behind this?'

'If not behind it, then at least willing to turn a blind eye — and perhaps to shield those responsible from the consequences, should their activities ever come to light.'

Jay nodded thoughtfully. 'Worryingly plausible. Or, it's the responsibility of some group who felt they had power enough in themselves to ignore the general disapprobation.'

'Maybe it's somebody like us, who falls under the jurisdiction of the Hidden Ministry and therefore is not, technically, acting illegally.'

'But if the Ministry only dates from the late seventeen hundreds, and the pups had already passed out of all knowledge by then, who bridged that gap?'

'Fair point. Perhaps the Ministry isn't the only organisation that hasn't enacted such laws. Mauf?'

'All officially recorded and recognised magickal organisations had agreed upon, and enacted such laws, by 1731,' said Mauf.

'Official?' said Jay. 'Are there unofficial ones?'

'It happens on occasion. They do not tend to last long, however.'

Which made sense. Setting up your own unsanctioned magickal state and proposing therefore to consider yourself above all magickal laws was not exactly widely supported behaviour. The usual consequence would be exactly as that enterprising band of spriggans discovered in 1727 — a speedy dispatch to prison, or something worse. It would be like buying your own island, declaring it an independent country, and expecting every other country in the world to nod, smile and pat you tolerantly on the head while you proceed to set up a factory for nuclear bombs on your tiny slice of paradise. This is not how it works.

But it doesn't stop people from occasionally trying.

'I wonder if some rogue magickal state has somehow gone undetected since the early eighteenth century?' I mused aloud.

'It isn't impossible,' said Jay. 'Not *quite*.'

'It is highly unlikely,' I agreed. 'And perhaps we're thinking too big now.'

'A smaller operation would have the greater chance of success,' said Jay. 'The bigger you are, the more noticeable you tend to be.'

'Some smaller operation with an incurable lust for treasure?' I suggested.

'Why else would you brave all dire consequences to keep a Goldnose handy?'

I nodded. 'I think Milady is right. Somebody needs to have a quiet talk with the spriggans.'

VALERIE NEEDED TO HAVE a quiet talk with Mauf, too, and so did Miranda. His casual revelation that the Dappledok Dell had been responsible for at least eight rare and desirable species of beasts required immediate investigation. I left the book at the Library, pausing only to relay enough of our findings to thoroughly electrify our sedate and dignified Boss Librarian. So energised was she, she almost tore the book right out of my hands.

I left them chatting cosily together, or so I hoped. Knowing Val, it would soon turn into an interrogation.

My next plan was to hustle back up to Milady's tower to relay Mauf's findings — and to see if the guide she had mentioned was here yet. I wanted to be on the road already, for little good ever comes of delaying something important. The sooner we talked to the spriggans of Dappledok, the better.

But I was distracted — twice.

I was halfway up the main stairs when I heard Miranda's voice calling me. I turned back. She had just come through the great doors leading into the east wing and was hastening towards me, her blonde hair half out of its ponytail as usual and a besmeared white coat over her jumper and jeans. A little dog trotted at her heels, and in spite of everything it still took me a moment to recognise my pup.

'What do you think?' said Mir, a bit breathlessly, as she came up to me.

I gazed at the pup. Instead of gold, her fur was now chocolate brown dappled liberally with purple, and there was no trace of the little horn that had adorned her forehead. She now had two horns instead, slightly thicker ones, nestled behind each of her pointed ears. Her nose had shrunk, and turned to an unobtrusive black colour.

In other words, she was a gorhound.

'Wow,' I said intelligently. 'That's amazing.'

Miranda nodded. 'They're good, aren't they?' she said, presumably referring to whichever of our illusionists had worked on the pup.

'Amazing,' I said again. So amazing, in fact, that for a brief, wild moment I wondered whether some switcheroo hadn't been performed, and the tiny Goldnose wasn't now languishing in some hidden nook in the east wing while I was fobbed off with a different creature altogether.

I squashed those ideas very quickly. What reason did I have to distrust Mir? None whatsoever. The illusionists really were that good, that was all.

When the gorhound puppy trotted up to me and rubbed herself all over my leg, my doubts vanished altogether. 'Hi, pup,' I said, and bent to pat her.

'Pup?' said Miranda. 'Doesn't she have a name?'

I know I have been referring to her as *my* pup for a while now, but I knew full well that she was no such thing. She was under my care for a little while, that was all, and if she had taken an obvious shine to me, well — what did that matter? No one was going to leave so rare, so valuable and so, er, *illegal* a beast with me for very long.

So I had not had the presumption to name her. It seemed wiser, somehow. If I did not name her, maybe I could refrain from getting too attached to her.

Hah.

'Pup works just fine,' I said, declining to explain all of this to Miranda.

I think she understood anyway, though, for she gave me a smile of unexpected sympathy and said, 'Perhaps it does, at that.'

It occurred to me that Miranda had probably been in the same situation over and over again. How many beasts had she bred and raised herself, or rescued and tenderly restored to health, only to have to relinquish them into someone else's possession? Or back into the wild? She would grow used to it, I supposed — to a degree. Her attachment to animals of all kinds was legendary at Home, after all.

Miranda gave me a salute and dashed off again, leaving the pup trailing around at my heels. We barely managed to climb four stairs between us that time before I heard the double doors of the front hall swing ponderously open, admitting a blaze of sunshine from outside. I say *heard* because they open with a groaning noise indicative of rusted hinges. They don't have rusted hinges, of course; the House is far too well-maintained to permit of that. But no amount of persuasion, oil-based or otherwise, can convince the doors to stop announcing each new visitor with some unpromising noise or another. I've long since concluded that House does it on purpose. If any building could be supposed to have a sense of humour, it would be ours.

Anyway, when the doors groan like that — or squeal, or cackle, choke — it means someone of note has arrived, so I stopped and went back down the stairs yet again.

I might have been planning to go forward to meet who-ever it was, but I swiftly revised all ideas of that kind and stayed firmly put. One judges it prudent, you know, with some visitors.

This one was most definitely of that kind. He was so tall, he had to stoop a long way to fit through the enormous doors, and he did not appear to find that an amusing process at all. He made it into the hall with some effort and stood, his short white hair brushing the high ceiling, looking down upon us puny humans with eyes the size of dinner plates.

All right, maybe not dinner plates. Afternoon tea plates, though, for certain. You could easily eat scones off those bright blue eyeballs.

He wore a long robe of blue cloth embroidered in gold, a white coat over the top, and (more puzzlingly, considering the weather) a pair of blue gloves. In other words, he made not the smallest effort to look like he belonged in any part of the modern world — but then, why should he? He was the size of about six humans put together.

'Giant,' I said faintly.

'So I see,' said Jay from behind me, startling me, for I had not noticed his approach. 'Do we often get giants stopping by?'

I had to think for a minute before I could remember the last time. At least five years ago. 'Nope,' I said succinctly.

'Right, then.'

The giant gave a long, windy sigh and said in lugubrious tones, 'Why must the doors always be so small?'

I pondered that. House is perfectly capable of adjusting proportions at need — be it of windows, chairs, or, indeed, doors. That it had not chosen to do so — and, further, that it had chosen to announce the arrival of this giant with so peculiarly unattractive a groaning noise — suggested to me that House did not altogether approve of our visitor.

Interesting.

Jay and I were not the only Society employs standing, frozen with surprise, in the hall. The giant surveyed the lot of us one by one, and when nobody spoke, he said: 'I am here to see Milady.'

There was no conceivable way he was going to fit in Milady's tower.

'Er,' said Jay in an undertone. 'That's going to be interesting.'

But of course, Milady had anticipated this. 'Welcome, Lord Garrogin,' she suddenly said from somewhere disconcertingly close to my head. 'We have been looking forward to your arrival.'

This, too, was unusual, and I could only answer Jay's questioning stare with a shrug. Yes, it was also a long time since Milady had been known to manifest (sort of) anywhere other than her tower. Yes, that probably meant nothing good either.

What can you do.

'Wonder if he's our guide or the Truthseeker?' whispered Jay.

'The latter,' I said instantly, and hoped I was right. Spriggans are not very tall. I collected that our guide was meant to be someone the spriggan courts might feel more comfortable associating with than a couple of humans, and I couldn't imagine their welcoming the arrival of so vast a being as Lord Garrogin in any such spirit.

I was swiftly proved right, for Milady's voice crisply announced: 'Consultations will shortly begin. Cordelia Vesper and Jay Patel to the Audience Chamber, please.'

That's Milady for you. For one thing, "Convention Chamber" is far too modern a term for her. She prefers "Audience Chamber," as though those summoned were to be presented to some manner of monarch. For another, "consultations" sounds so much nicer than "inquisition", doesn't it?

'Why are we first?' whispered Jay to me as we dutifully headed for the Chamber of Gorgeousness.

'Probably because we're supposed to be on our way to Sprigganland already.'

'If our guide's here.'

'He or she probably is, or they're imminently expected. Milady doesn't waste time.'

'As evidenced by the prompt appearance of Lord Garrogin, Giant, from Parts Unknown.'

'Precisely.'

Lord Garrogin was nowhere in evidence when we arrived at the Audience/Convention Chamber. Milady had probably taken him off for an initial briefing, and was overseeing the pouring of hot chocolate down his gargantuan throat at that very moment. The enormous Inquisition Room (as I would now have to think of it) was echoingly empty, though I was heartened to see that refreshments had been provided: the long, crystalline table running down the centre of the marble-floored hall was absolutely smothered in the refined sorts of dishes that come with polished silver covers. I knew they had tasty things inside them because the air was filled with an enticing medley of aromas.

This circumstance puzzled more than pleased Jay, however. 'That seems... excessive,' he said, nodding his chin at the laden table.

'This is Milady, remember.'

'And?'

I pulled out a velvet-cushioned chair at the bottom of the table and sat on it. 'Well,' I said, stretching. 'There are probably two reasons for it. For one, Milady's really very kind-hearted. I suppose she cannot predict how long each interview will take, and she would hate for us to get hungry while we suffer Lord Garrogin's interrogation.'

Jay sat down next to me. 'Hence enough food for about two hundred people. I suppose the dishes keep everything warm?'

'Undoubtedly.'

'All right. And what's the other reason?'

'Milady is almost as devious as she is kind. Well-fed people are comfortable people, and food puts almost everyone at their ease. The comfier you are, the less guarded you are, and that is probably going to make his lordship's job a bit easier.'

'Remind me never to underestimate Milady.'

'Everyone underestimates Milady.'

Jay chewed his lip. 'But doesn't interrogation make for uneasy people anyway?'

'Depends how good Lord Garrogin is.'

The heavy thud of approaching footsteps announced the arrival of our interrogator, and I wondered whether we ought to stand up. I decided not to.

Jay didn't. And if he was going to politely get to his feet then that sort of meant I had to, as well. I stifled a sigh as I hauled my bones out of the chair again, and watched Lord Garrogin's ponderous approach with, despite my sanguine words, a faint flicker of apprehension. He did make an imposing appearance, no doubt about that. And hadn't I just said that Milady was devious? She had told Jay and me that we were not under suspicion, but that, too, might have been a ploy to put us at our ease.

I wondered distantly when I had become so fretful, and banished those thoughts. Time to focus.

'My lord,' I said as Garrogin reached us.

He nodded to us both, and made his slow way to the head of the table. The chair there was no larger than the ones Jay and I had been sitting in, but that did not last. As the giant approached, the chair twitched and swelled to four times its former size, and it wasn't finished at that. Formerly a sleek, armless dining chair of some silver-coloured wood, it thickened and stretched until its silvery frame bore more of a throne-like appearance, complete with tall arm rests. Its blueish cushions became a rich purple just shy of royal in tone, and it even developed some kind of diamond jewel at the top of its arched back.

House had been Spoken To, I guessed. His Lordship was evidently to be pampered, and Milady had insisted. If there was a touch of the satirical about the excesses of that throne, who was I to judge?

Lord Garrogin — was he in fact some kind of minor princeling, out in giant territory? He could be, I supposed, and that would explain the throne — Lord Garrogin sat down, and the majestic chair bore his weight without a whimper. He sat for a moment looking thoughtfully at us.

Jay and I stared back.

6

'Please have a seat,' the giant finally said. 'Covers, please.'

This last made no sense to me whatsoever, but before I could ask for an explanation, two of the silver dishes shivered and spat their covers into the air, where they promptly vanished. The two dishes hastened to set themselves before us, and I noted with approval (but not much surprise) that mine contained three items: a piece of carrot cake, a custard slice, and a cup of chocolate. Three of my very favourite things.

I peeked at Jay's: it had a fat samosa, a plate of chips, and a cup of tea... no, the contents of the little cup were far too dark for tea.

'Since when are you a coffee drinker?' I whispered to him.

He shot me a vaguely guilty look. 'I like tea as well,' he said defensively.

'Traitor.'

He flicked a chip at me.

We had ended up seated within easy talking distance of Lord Garrogin, but not so close that I could see what his dishes were. I was disappointed. Food is a bit of an interest of mine — big surprise, right? — and I was curious about what kinds of things giants might like to eat.

'Cordelia Vesper,' said Garrogin. 'And Jay Patel. I understand you work together?'

'As of a few weeks ago,' I confirmed, picking up the shiny silver fork that came with my plate and tucking into the cake. 'He's our new Waymaster, and I am training him to join the Acquisitions Division.'

'Tell me about Acquisitions,' said Garrogin. He had a deep, soothing voice, and I genuinely did feel calmed by it. The flutter of nerves in my belly dissipated.

'Well, we are the — the public arm of the Society, I suppose,' I said. 'We track down and retrieve artefacts, treasures, trinkets and curiosities, books, beasts, talismans — anything really — that might be under threat, and make sure they get where they need to go. Sometimes that's here, sometimes elsewhere.'

'We fix problems, too,' Jay said. 'It's not just retrieval. On my first assignment with Ves, we went after a pair of stolen alikats and discovered a disease infesting half the dormant Troll Enclaves in the country. Took a bit to resolve that one.'

'And how did you resolve it?' said Garrogin, in the same even tone.

'In the end, we had to go all the way to Farringale,' said Jay, dipping a chip in ketchup.

That prompted a small reaction from our giant interrogator. 'You entered Farringale? What did you do there?'

So we told him that story, and that got us onto the tale of Bill the Book. By the time we had finished telling him about all of that, my cakes and chocolate were gone, and Jay had wiped his plate clean of chips, ketchup and samosas alike.

Garrogin hadn't touched his dishes at all.

'You have had a lively time of it,' he observed.

'It's never a dull job,' I agreed. 'Though to be fair, it's not usually quite *that* exciting.'

Lord Garrogin nodded thoughtfully, and at last — at *last* — he selected some small morsel of something from his plate and consumed it with ponderous slowness. 'What drew you to the Society?' he asked, looking at Jay.

The question came a bit out of the blue, so I could not blame Jay for looking a trifle startled. But he answered quickly. 'It's legendary, for one thing. Everyone here is really committed to the preservation of our magickal heritage, and... well, without Milady and her recruits, we'd have lost a lot of irreplaceable things by now. That's more important to me than anything. And then my parents both worked here, before I was born. They always had great stories to tell. I never really wanted anything else.'

That interested me, for I'd never heard that Jay's mother and father had been employees here. But Garrogin did not seem disposed to follow up that line of enquiry. Instead he said, with probably deceptive blandness, 'Not even for a much higher salary?'

'The Society pays as much as I need,' said Jay.

Garrogin nodded, and turned his sharp blue gaze upon me. 'And why do you stay, Cordelia?'

'It's Ves,' I said. 'Cordelia makes me feel like a porcelain doll. I stay for all the reasons Jay just said. There is nothing more important I could do with my time and my skills, is there? And I love the variety, the challenge... no two days are ever the same. I once regretted not being assigned to the Library, but much as I love books and research, I'd probably be getting bored by now.'

Lord Garrogin's eyes narrowed the merest fraction, and my stomach tightened. What had I said to prompt that reaction? But the expression faded, and he actually smiled at us both. Not much, but there was a definite curving of his lips. 'Thank you,' he said, in a tone of dismissal. 'It has been an enlightening conversation.'

He did not appear in any way displeased, so I tried not to conclude that this comment boded ill, and got up from my chair. 'It was a pleasure to meet you,' I said politely.

He inclined his head to us both. 'We will meet again.'

Would we? That definitely sounded ominous.

Jay and I exchanged identical looks of mild concern, and beat a hasty retreat.

THE "CONSULTATIONS" WENT ON all day, but there was no news to be had as to how they were progressing. Jay and I wandered listlessly about the common room for a while, and when neither word nor orders arrived, we decided to arrange our own entertainment.

Extra equipment required: one Valerie, one Mauf, one Library of Dreams.

Objective: find out more about the Dappledok Dell, the spriggan courts, and anything else that seemed pertinent.

We arrived at Val's enormous desk to find her getting very cosy with Mauf.

She had the book laid before her on a thick cushion, un-opened. Mauf's cover was glinting with light again; I was rapidly learning that this was a sign of interest with him, perhaps even excitement. Val had a notepad beside her and a pen in one hand, and she was furiously writing notes, one finger tapping frenetically upon Mauf's gorgeous leather cover.

She looked up when Jay and I walked in. 'This is amazing,' she said. 'The library has nothing about any of this. *Nothing.*'

'The Dappledok beasts?' I asked, pulling up a chair. Sitting on the audience side of Valerie's desk always feels odd. Val's chair is handsome, and elevated on a slight pedestal besides, so she's very much looking down on anybody seated on the other side. Valerie herself can be a touch imposing, too — not that she isn't friendly, of course. But she's a tall, majestic sort of woman with perfect posture and incredibly well-groomed hair, and while she's always been a staunch friend to me, some part of her manner can sometimes feel a bit... brisk, shall we say? It feels a bit like taking a meeting with the approachable but mildly awe-inspiring CEO of some vast, important company.

I cannot say that I mind, though. Val is the undisputed queen of the library, a post she has thoroughly earned, and she deserves every scrap of status that comes with it.

Anyway. 'There were eight different species,' Val said to me. 'Each more remarkable than the last, and I don't say that lightly. Irreplaceable. I cannot believe that so many of them were permitted to pass out of existence — nay, not permitted, but forced to!'

Jay politely broke in upon this discourse. 'How many of them have been banned?'

'Four, of the eight,' she said promptly, then paused. 'Right, Mauf?'

'Correct, madam.'

Apparently my book and Valerie were getting along swimmingly, if one of them was already on a first-name basis. Mauf had a bit of formality to get over. I'd give it about... twenty-five years.

Valerie consulted her notes, flipping back a page or two. 'The Goldnoses, as they were colloquially known, though their correct name was — never mind. Too much detail, Val. They were banned because they facilitated the life of crime far more than anybody was comfortable with. Another species had a talent for lifting curses, which you might think would be a good thing, unless they were being used to circumvent the kinds of curses that have been laid down for good reason — you know the kind of thing, Ves.'

I did. That chamberpot, for example. I had cursed it so that it would do a few, er, rather unpleasant things to anybody who contrived to get into it without my permission. We call that a curse, because it's essentially dark magic, but its use for the protection of personal property (among other things) is common, and widely supported.

'A useful creature to have alongside your Goldnose,' I remarked.

'Extremely. A third was forbidden purely because it could never be cured of its tendency to go wild and bite everybody within range, and since its fangs were venomous this was considered undesirable.'

Jay snorted.

'And finally, the fourth. A sweet little thing, as much like a kitten as the Goldnoses are like adorable little puppies. Only it was bred for its milk, which happens to be hallucinogenic in very bad ways.'

'Hallucinogenic?!' I echoed. 'What was that about?'

Valerie shot me a look. 'Why does anybody manufacture drugs, Ves?'

'Fair point.'

'And the other four?' Jay asked.

'Two of them are on the endangered species list, and the other two became so common that nobody remembers — or cares — where they came from anymore. All of them possess, at most, minor and harmless abilities.'

I thought that over. 'Interesting array of beasties.'

'Isn't it?' Val agreed. 'To the credit of Dappledok, the four that were never banned were pretty terrific achievements. But the *other* four? Odd mixture.'

'I wonder what they were after.'

Valerie shrugged. 'Possibly there was no master plan, they were just experimenting. Exercising their powers. That kind of thing.'

'Then again,' said Jay, 'it has been said that spriggans are known for a love of all things gold.'

Valerie pursed her lips. 'In the same way that humans are, probably. Collectively, we're powerfully influenced by material wealth, but that doesn't make all of us robbers and thieves.'

Jay inclined his head, conceding the point.

'So who was responsible for these creatures?' I asked. 'If Dappledok is anything like most Dells, it's fairly sizeable, and a lot of different people live there. Or did, once upon a time. All we've heard so far is that "spriggans" made the Goldnoses, but that's a broad category.'

'It is far too broad, though it is true enough. Mauf?'

The book glittered with enthusiasm. 'The Dappledok Dell had two main neighbourhoods: one inhabited, predominantly, by spriggans, and the other home to a large community of brownies. Scattered about across the rest was quite the array of other beings, including a few humans. I speak of its heyday, which lasted for much of the seventeenth century. It declined somewhat thereafter, and today it is known as a quiet, reclusive Dell rarely open to outsiders.'

'And the spriggans?' I prompted.

'I am getting to that,' said Mauf, calmly but firmly.

I was abashed. 'Sorry.'

Mauf made a throat-clearing noise. Somehow. 'The spriggans of Dappledok were a mixture of multiple tribes, but the most powerful of them were the Redclovers, who founded a school at Dappledok in 1372. The establishment grew to considerable size over the next two centuries, and was held in such high repute that people travelled to Dappledok from all over Britain to attend. They taught a range of magickal techniques and theories but their specialisation, as I am sure you will not be surprised to hear, was all matters relating to the capture, care, breeding and use of magickal beasts. It is that school, and its attendant workshops, which produced all eight of the species I have previously discussed with Valerie.'

The Redclover School. Interesting.

Jay spoke up. 'Where did you learn all this, Bill? I mean, Mauf?'

'I came across it during my time at the Library of Farringale.'

'Did you absorb *all* the knowledge of that place?'

'To my shame, no. It was not possible to properly converse with those books placed too far away from my shelf. I would estimate that I was only able to exchange information with approximately seven thousand books.'

There was a short silence following this extraordinary statement, during which (judging from their faces) Jay and Valerie were thinking much the same thing as I was.

Seven thousand??!

Had they all been lost volumes, full of information we no longer had access to? If so, Valerie was going to be very, very busy for about the next twelve lifetimes.

Anyway. I forcibly dragged my reeling mind back to the point at hand, albeit with some difficulty. 'Redclover,' I said aloud.

'Spriggans,' Jay added helpfully.

'Dappledok beasts. One ancient mystery at a time, right?'

Jay said, 'Right,' but in tones of deep regret with which I could only sympathise.

My phone buzzed.

I grabbed it from my pocket. 'Ves,' I said.

Unbelievably, and unprecedentedly, Milady's voice echoed into my ear. 'Mabyn Redclover has just arrived at the front hall, Ves. I am much engaged with Lord Garrogin at present, and since Mabyn is to be your guide to Dappledok, may I ask you and Jay to meet her?'

I swiftly agreed, and put away my phone. 'A lady's arrived to see Jay and me,' I announced.

'A lady?' asked Jay.

'Her name is Mabyn.'

Jay gave me a quizzical frown.

'Redclover,' I said with a grin.

Jay's eyes widened, and he shot out of his chair. 'Going.'

We went.

'Keep me posted!' called Valerie after us.

I turned around long enough to make a cross-my-heart gesture, and... and I noticed Mauf still lying before Valerie.

I ran back to grab him.

'Ves! I am not finished!'

'Sorry,' I said with total sincerity, but not at all deterred. 'We're going to need him.'

7

JAY HAD NEVER MET a spriggan before.

Neither had I, in fact, but since it was my sacred duty to be the knowledgeable, world-wise one, I had no intention of telling him that. I went forward to meet Mabyn Red-clover with a practiced air of confident ease, and bid her warmly welcome to the Society.

Not that there was anything in her appearance to disgust, or even to disconcert. True, her head was a little overlarge for her body, but she was well-dressed and impeccably groomed and I respect that. She was a foot or so shorter than me (so, in other words, *very* short), and appeared to be of advanced age, judging from her wizened skin and white hair. She wore a sixties-style two-piece suit, jacket and skirt perfectly matched, with low heels and gold earrings. She hadn't gone for the beehive hair, slightly to my disappointment; instead, she had a nicely coiffed bob. We arrived in the hall to find her standing in the middle of it, looking around with obvious interest.

She took off her gloves when I went to greet her, and shook my hand warmly. 'Mabyn Redclover,' she introduced herself. 'I'm with the Ministry. Department of Forbidden Magicks.'

My eyebrows rose. Milady had reached rather high, and was it a coincidence that Ms. Redclover was an expert in magickal misdemeanours? I imagined not.

Jay and I introduced ourselves.

'Pleasure,' she said briskly. 'You are the two I was invited to meet, are you? What may I do for you?'

'Any connection at all to the Redclovers of Dappledok?' asked Jay.

A faint grimace flickered over her lips, and was gone. 'Once. A long time ago.'

I suppose you would distance yourself from family connections like that, in her line of work. But I wondered, then, why she had never changed her name.

Jay nodded. 'Has Milady described our current situation to you?'

'An outline only. A Dappledok beast has been found?'

'One of the questionable ones.' Jay proceeded to fill in the details. I, meanwhile, tried not to look as though I had the creature in question tucked into the bag hanging from my left shoulder, and hoped that the pup would not choose this of all possible moments to stick her head out for some air.

She didn't, but Ms. Redclover's eyes settled upon me with a shrewd expression I could not quite like. 'You have the pup here?' she said.

I sighed, and lifted the flap of my bag. I did so with some trepidation, in case Ms. Redclover, of Forbidden Magicks, should decide to confiscate her — or worse. But she only looked briefly into the bag, noted the dark shape of the pup curled up in the bottom, and withdrew. 'Disguised?'

'Yes.'

'Excellent illusion.'

I smiled, uncertain. Chit-chat? Surely she must feel some disapproval. 'There were three of them in the cottage,' I elaborated. 'Two failed to survive. We believe there must be some manner of secret breeding programme going on somewhere, and we'd like to get to the bottom of it.'

'So would we,' said Mabyn Redclover, with a thin smile. 'Milady has assigned you to assist me, so we will be working together for a time. I trust that will be agreeable?'

I felt a little surprise. Assigned to work with Mabyn? Had she not been sent to serve as our guide? Just who was in charge here?

It was typical of Milady to couch the situation in rather different terms to us, but the melancholy truth was: Ministry employees outranked us, especially the higher ups. And Ms. Redclover had every appearance of being one of those, from her manicured nails to her air of business-like efficiency. She was the kind of person who confidently expects to be obeyed without question, and that spoke volumes.

'Well, actually—' said Jay.

I coughed, interrupting him. 'That will be fine,' I told her. 'We are ready to depart for Dappledok at once, if that is acceptable to you.'

'Quite.' She looked at Jay. 'You are a Waymaster, yes?'

'I am.'

She nodded, and took — I kid you not — a plastic rain-hood out of a pocket of her suit. This she unfolded, and placed carefully over her perfectly coiffed hair, tying the strings under her chin. 'Right away, then,' she said briskly.

Jay looked at me, and I shrugged. I hoped my shrug would convey something along the lines of, *best to do as the nice lady says,* but to Jay it apparently said something more like *I have no idea, it's your problem*, for his mouth tightened, and he walked off with only a brief nod for Ms. Redclover.

She fell in beside me as I wandered after Jay, fussily adjusting the sit of her rain-hood. 'Terse young man, isn't he?' she said in an undertone.

'He's only been with us for a few weeks yet. I think he's still finding his feet.'

'Ahh,' she said wisely. 'I remember those days.'

I was tempted to ask her how long it had been since she'd felt young and uncertain, but wisely restrained the impulse.

'You were lucky to get him,' she added after a moment.

'We were. He's a highly talented Waymaster. One of the best, I understand, though you'd never hear him say it.'

'The Ministry wanted to bid for him, but Milady was too fast. One or two people were mighty displeased about that.'

My mouth twitched, though I managed to suppress the smug smile that threatened to emerge. 'I am sure Milady was duly apologetic.'

'Most apologetic. Not at all sorry, of course, but most apologetic.'

I did smile at that. Plastic hats or no, I began to feel that Ms. Redclover and I might just get along.

Ms. Redclover went through the Winds of the Ways with her hands carefully clamped over her hair. I privately thought it absurd, until she emerged at a windy henge atop a cliff somewhere in (presumably) Cornwall with her hair intact and I... didn't.

As I nonchalantly shook out my tangled curls I reminded myself that perfect hair isn't everything.

'So,' I said to Jay with a brilliant smile. 'Er, whereabouts are we?'

'Cornwall.'

I looked around. We stood high up over the water on rocky ground covered in feathery green grasses. Great boulders lay everywhere, protruding pugnaciously from the earth, and the sun shone gorgeously over a patchwork of meadows stretching away into the distance. 'Edifying.'

He smiled faintly at me, and pointed over my shoulder. 'That's the sea.'

I stared out over the expanse of glittering blue water. 'So that's what the sea looks like.'

'Watery.'

'Very.'

With a tiny sigh, he said, 'We are as far west in England as you can get, and a long way south. We're somewhere along what they now call the Penwith Heritage Coast, which means we are smack in the middle of spriggan country, and the entrance to the Dappledok Dell is not far from here.'

I gave him a tiny salute. 'Thank you, Captain Geography.'

'You are welcome, Captain History.'

I had half expected him to call me Captain Sparkle or something, but I liked his alternative. 'I've never been to Cornwall,' I admitted.

'Never?' He looked incredulous. 'I thought you'd been in Acquisitions for ten years.'

'I have, but somehow I never ended up in Cornwall.'

'Interesting.

Ms. Redclover gave a slight cough. 'The day marches on,' she observed.

It did, at that. It must be well past noon already, and Jay and I were bantering the afternoon away. 'Sorry,' I said hastily. 'Lead on, Jay?'

He led on. We wended our way around the coastline for half an hour or so, and I had cause to be thankful that I had chosen a jeans-and-flat-shoes combination that morning. I wondered if Ms. Redclover might be regretting her shoe choices a bit, but she trudged on with unimpaired composure and seemed unaffected.

I wondered if her unruffled attitude was Ministry-issue, or innate.

After a while, Jay stopped at what must be a specific point in the largely featureless landscape, though I could see no way to tell. We had gone down a sandy incline to a beach littered with stones, and the cliff rose above us, jagged and rocky and just a bit forbidding, if it hadn't been for the balmy, sunny weather. He stood staring at the rock wall. 'Ms. Redclover?' he said after a while.

'Mabyn, please, Mr. Patel.'

He flashed her one of his charming smiles. 'Jay, then.'

She inclined her head.

'I believe we will need your help to get in.'

Mabyn stepped forward, lips pursed. 'Likely, yes. Dappledok closed its doors to outsiders a long time ago, though never entirely. It *has* been a long time, however...' She let the sentence trail off and began to wander up and down the beach, her keen eyes scanning the rock for signs of... something? Jay and I stood, patiently waiting.

'Ah,' she finally said, and stepped forward. Lifting one thin hand, she knocked thrice upon the rock face and said something in a language I had never heard before.

'Ancient Cornish?' guessed Jay.

'Probably,' I whispered back.

Whatever it was she had said, it soon proved effective. A line of sea-green light snaked down the cliff face, and with the horrific groaning sound of grinding rock, a crack appeared, just wide enough for a spriggan — or indeed, a human — to pass through.

Mabyn went in, beckoning over her shoulder to the two of us.

'After you,' said Jay with a half-bow.

'I promise you, even I cannot manage to get lost between here and the cliff.' The distance was all of, what, twelve feet?

Jay grinned at me. 'I'd like to make sure.'

I stuck my tongue out at him, and followed after Mabyn. And into the Dappledok Dell went we, agog with curiosity (or maybe that last part was just me).

Well, let me tell you, my first glimpse of that ancient Dell was... a little bit of a let-down.

Not that it wasn't beautiful. It was, gloriously so. I have probably mentioned the tendency of the magickal Dells to look... well, magick-drenched. Everything practically glows with vitality and beauty, at least with those that are still thriving; the abandoned ones are a different matter. Dappledok wasn't abandoned. It glittered and glowed.

But it was exactly the same landscape as the one we had just left; in fact, it looked identical, save only for the extra blush of vibrancy to the blue-green water, and the sparkle to the sunlight. I don't know what I had been hoping for. Skies full of rainbows? Meadows chock-full of cute puppy-like creatures frolicking in the sunlight?

Ms. Redclover behaved like a native, for all her attempts to distance herself from her ancient familial home. She set off along the beach at a purposeful walk, with the air of a woman walking a long-familiar route. 'Dapplehaven is just around the corner,' she called over her shoulder.

'What is Dapplehaven?' I asked, hastening to catch up with her.

'The largest town in the Dell. The Redclover School is there.'

Straight to the point, hm? I smothered the desire to go for a long, exploratory hike, and dutifully trotted after Ms. Mabyn Redclover.

But we had not gone very far before three most unpromising things happened one after another.

First, it literally went dark. Not completely pitch, but the sun went pale and watery, like someone had turned down a dimmer switch.

Next, the magickal equivalent of a klaxon sounded from somewhere nearby. It sounds less like a car horn and more like an entire flock of griffins all screaming at once.

When a dark speck appeared on the horizon, I knew we were somewhat in trouble.

'This does not seem good,' said Jay, coming to a sudden halt, and warily eyeing the skies.

Ms. Redclover gave a huffy sigh, and fussed with her hair. 'Always so *prone* to overreaction. Some things never do change, do they?'

I was watching that dark speck in silence. It grew rapidly bigger, proving itself to be winged, with a snaky body and four legs. 'Yep,' I said as it drew nearer. 'Dragon.'

It wasn't all that big of a dragon, in fairness, but it was plenty big enough to ruin our collective day. As it swooped down upon us, jaws gaping, with purple fire streaming from between its fangs, Ms. Redclover shook her head with another huffy sigh and said, 'Oh, *Archibald.*'

8

'Who,' croaked Jay, eyes glued to the descending draconic menace, 'is Archibald?'

I wanted to ask much the same thing, but I had been too busy digging for my Wand. I had not yet got around to returning the Sunstone Wand to Stores after our last adventure, for which oversight (ahem) I was now heartily grateful.

Trouble is, I had not expected to encounter so direct a menace two minutes into the Dappledok Dell, and I had left it somewhere in the depths of my shoulder bag. The pup was sleeping on it, and was remarkably resistant to suggestion. 'Er,' I said, beginning to panic, my fingers scrabbling uselessly for any trace of cool gemstone beneath the pup's thick, fluffy fur. '*Duck!*'

We dived for the floor. The dragon swooped, claws extended, and mercifully missed all three of us.

Wait, no. No, it didn't. Jay and I had hit the floor, but Mabyn Redclover had stood her ground like an idiot, arms crossed, tutting the way Matron used to upon finding ten-year-old Ves reading her book by torchlight well after lights out. (I was a well-behaved child most of the time, I swear).

The dragon, unimpressed with this display of disapproval, scooped her up in its long, polished claws and flew away again.

Mabyn's voice drifted back to us along the balmy spring breeze. 'I will get this sorted out! Wait there.'

Jay and I could only watch, helpless, as the dragon dwindled into the distance, taking our guide with it.

'Well,' said Jay.

I hefted my bag. I had found the Wand by then, disturbing the pup in the process, and she was now sitting up, yawning, her ears perked as she looked around. 'Time to explore after all, then,' I said brightly.

Jay gave me his what-are-you-talking-about look. He does something odd and sceptical with his eyebrows. It's hard to describe. 'Don't you think we ought to help Mabyn?'

'Did she sound distressed to you?'

The what-the-hell face became a frown. 'No. Why didn't she sound distressed?'

'My guess is that the dragon's called Archibald. Or he belongs to someone else with that name.'

'Possibly not the first time she's travelled by dragon?' Jay surmised.

'Possibly not. Shall we go?'

'She said, "Wait there."'

'I know. I heard her.'

'We aren't doing that?'

'Did you especially want to?'

'We should.' Jay said this very gravely. 'She is effectively our boss for today.'

I put the Wand away again. 'All right, then.'

Time passed.

Jay, to his credit, did a champion job of pretending not to be stupefied with boredom. He wandered about, hands shoved into the pockets of his dark leather jacket, an expression of bland interest on his face as he inspected the same outcropping of tan-coloured rock about sixteen times over.

I sat cross-legged on a nearby boulder, the pup in my lap, and stared into space.

After about seven minutes of this, he said, nonchalantly, 'Maybe we could explore a little bit.'

'We could.'

'If we don't go too far?'

'Absolutely.'

'Do you want to lead?'

'Nope.'

He set off.

'Jay,' I said.

'What?'

'How about we go in generally the same direction as the dragon?'

He turned around, scowling. 'I did ask you if you wanted to lead.'

I hopped off my boulder, electing to keep the pup in my arms rather than let her run, and beamed at him. 'Just helping out.'

'It's not the worst idea,' he conceded.

My smile widened.

'Fine. You're right, we'll go this way.'

The dragon had flown off inland, more or less in the direction Mabyn Redclover had been going herself. I judged it likely, therefore, that the dragon (Archibald?) had come from Dapplehaven, and had probably returned there with Mabyn. Why we had been left out of this kidnapping party, I had no idea, though I wasn't about to complain. If I am going to fly, I will do it by winged horse, thank you very much. Or chair. Or, I suppose, airplane. Those are the only three options.

My hypothesis seemed sound, for after a half-hour's wending our way across the uneven curves of a stony hillside feathered with bracken and heath, the walls of a little town came into view surmounting the very top of the peak. At least, it appeared to be of limited size at first, but as we drew nearer, it became clear that the settlement extended much farther back than had initially been apparent. The walls were taller than Jay, and built from a reddish-tan stone obviously hewn from the local hills. Those buildings we could see were mostly constructed from the same material, as well as sturdy oak and pine wood. To my eyes, they looked diminutive, being of course the homes of spriggans and other beings built along smaller lines than humans. But they did not lack vision. Neatly constructed from smooth bricks, with sloping, tiled roofs and mullioned windows, they towered over the town walls, most of them built at least four storeys high.

If this was Dapplehaven, it was a prosperous place despite its reclusive habits.

One particularly tall tower rose in the centre, a round-walled construct made from a much paler stone than the rest, and fitted with a variety of peculiar windows, every one of them a different shape. Its top was crowned with a huge nest made out of what looked like lengths of coloured cloth. It made a cheery sight, in spite of its probable purpose.

I pointed it out to Jay. 'Suppose that's Archibald's house?'

'Looks dragon-sized,' he agreed.

Gradually, I became aware of a problem. Walls there were, but it occurred to me that I had caught no glimpse whatsoever of a gate, or a door, or an archway, or even a window, through which Jay and I might enter the town. We walked on, following the curve of the walls around and around, but no sign of an entrance did we find.

At length, Jay stopped. 'We can't walk around the entire town. If there was going to be anything obvious like a gate, it would have been on the side we approached from — facing the entrance.'

'Are you sure? They stopped taking visitors from Cornwall many years ago.'

'And then moved the gate? Did you see anything on the walls that looked like a bricked-up doorway?'

'No,' I conceded.

'It's got to be a hidden entrance, like the door in the cliff face which only Mabyn could find.'

I heaved a sigh. 'Why do Dells always have to make things so difficult.'

'Because they hate you.'

'Thanks.'

'And me, and the entire unmagicked population of Britain especially.'

'Not altogether unreasonable of them,' I murmured, thinking of many instances of persecution, theft, abuse and other such joys the magicker populations of our country had previously endured. Not to mention that the threat of exposure held more perils now than it ever had before. Imagine what would happen if some well-meaning but excitable non-magicker person discovered somewhere like Dappledok Dell — and managed to prove its existence to the rest of the world. Okay, we're past the point where anybody would be likely to come down here with the torches and the pitchforks and burn the residents at the stake. Instead? Hordes of people would come down here with their Canon 70Ds and their camping gear and their Harry Potter t-shirts and the whole thing would become a theme park inside of about a week.

'So, hidden door,' I said to the wall before me. 'Fun.'

'Maybe it's back where we started,' said Jay. 'Near the portal to Cornwall.'

'Could be.'

'It's probably operated by a word, or a phrase. Something in Ancient Cornish, or whatever it was that Mabyn was speaking.'

'One of the spriggan languages, possibly,' I mused.

'One of them?'

'They have many dialects. Just like humans, isn't that odd?'

He grimaced at me. 'All right, sorry. Do you happen to speak any of them?'

'No. Not having expected to end up in spriggan country, I specialised in old English and Court Algatish, which is the official language of Trolldom at the moment. I dabbled a bit in one or two of the goblin and elf tongues, but I never made much progress with those.'

Jay stared at me, bemused. 'You speak Algatish?'

'Not fluently, but not too badly.'

He visibly shook himself. 'Er. So, we aren't going to make much progress with the door if neither of us can speak any of the likely languages.'

'Gosh, whatever shall we do.' I reached out a hand and rapped politely upon the wall.

'Knock?' said Jay incredulously. 'That's the plan?'

'Just wait.'

It took about thirty-five seconds.

'Who goes there?' snapped an irritable female voice, and a face shimmered into view. She was almost as wizened in appearance as Mabyn, though she was much more addicted to jewellery, and she wore bright lipstick.

'I've always wanted to say *who goes there*,' I whispered to Jay. 'I'd say it with a bit more bombast, though.'

'Er,' said Jay. 'We're from the Society for Magickal Heritage, based in Yorkshire. We are here on an urgent matter of business.'

'We had a guide,' I added helpfully. 'Mabyn Redclover. A dragon made off with her.'

The woman's brows snapped down. 'Wait there,' she grunted, and the vision dissolved.

'I was tempted to say "We come in peace,"' Jay remarked.

'You could have. I doubt she would have got the reference.'

'Next time. So is this how it normally works?'

'What?'

'You just... knock?'

I shrugged. 'It works more often than it doesn't. The Dells certainly don't encourage tourism, but it's not like you're in danger of being put to death for setting foot in here. And she must realise we had to have qualified help to get this far.'

The woman herself appeared shortly afterwards. A line of green fire snaked its way up the wall, tracing the shape of an elegant and surprisingly tall archway, and the stonework within apparently vanished. Our grumpy receptionist stood revealed in all the glory of an early Edwardian tea gown in heliotrope silk, a sash tied round her nipped-in waist. Fashions don't always advance much once a Dell closes its doors to the outside world. Then again, some people just like to dress vintage.

'Mabyn Redclover is currently unavailable,' she snapped.

'We guessed that,' I said.

'Is she all right?' Jay put in.

'Perfectly. What do you think Archibald was going to do, eat her? Credentials please.'

We flashed our Society symbols. Mine has the unicorn superimposed over the three crossed wands, but Jay has only the wands so far. He hasn't yet had time to pick a unique identifier.

I might as well add: no, these are not fakeable. It's like the magickal equivalent of that special paper and holographic stuff they use on cash money to make it hard (if not completely impossible) to fake. No one can use my symbol but me. Val and I tried, once, to fake each other's symbols. The results were not pretty. My face hurt for three weeks afterwards.

'Fine. Come in.' The Edwardian spriggan turned her back on us and stalked back through the archway, which promptly began to display signs that the stone blocks were returning.

'Quick.' I grabbed Jay and dragged him through the arch, just as stone rippled back into place with a nasty grinding sound. Nice if we'd got stuck halfway through when that happened.

'Hospitable,' Jay muttered.

'Habit,' I countered. 'I don't think they get groups here very often.'

The town of Dapplehaven had all the hallmarks of an old, old settlement: narrow streets winding every which way, betraying the absolute absence of a town planner; old stone or timber-framed houses with crumbling facades built onto the front in updated styles; an occasional old well, which may or may not be still in use; doors with the doorknobs in the middle, instead of on the left side; uneven stone-cobbled streets; all of that kind of thing. They had updated a bit, though, for they had wrought iron streetlamps in that charming, late-Victorian style (ornate), and a suspiciously twentieth-century-looking wheelbarrow parked in somebody's front garden (not so ornate).

Our new guide escorted us through several winding streets and at last entered a tall, skinny building with an unfortunate unsteady appearance. By which I mean, it was distinctly leaning at the top.

This did not appear to trouble our guide, who took us through a featureless entrance hall and up three flights of stairs. She shoved open a door in the subsequent hallway and ushered us into it.

Mabyn Redclover sat there on a hard oak chair. Her suit was torn in three places, and — alas! — her hair had very much come a-cropper. She was also missing a shoe.

'Your assistants,' said the Edwardian woman.

'Thanks, Doryty,' said Mabyn sourly. 'I am sure you gave them one of your warm welcomes.'

'Naturally. Wait a moment.'

She left us with Mabyn.

'What got into Archibald?' said Jay, sitting down beside her.

That won him a faint smile. 'We go a long way back.'

'Really? He didn't look all that friendly.'

Mabyn looked away. 'I did not leave on quite the best terms. Those who have the care of Archibald these days were not best pleased to see me back.'

'What about Doryty?' I put in.

'Doryty Redclover. A cousin on my mother's side.'

'Good relationship there?'

'Not really.'

Milady's knowledgeable, well-connected guide turned out to be about the least popular person in Dappledok? Great.

I was in for a headache.

9

I SUPPOSE WE SHOULDN'T have been surprised. Mabyn Redclover had aligned herself with precisely the type of organisation — and the very department thereof — most likely to be opposed and despised by those who remained loyal to the goals of the Redclover school. She had become a person who made a point of getting in the way of projects like the Redclovers', curtailing their options and limiting their prospects for reasons with which they apparently disagreed. If you were not disposed to consider those kinds of laws as justified, Mabyn's choices would tend to look rather like defection to the enemy.

I wondered what kinds of things they were getting up to at the school these days.

'We need to pay a visit to the Redclover School,' I said.

Mabyn gave me an exasperated look. 'It has been forty years since I left. I thought they might have got over their anger by now, but apparently not. They aren't going to let us anywhere near that school.'

'Not you, perhaps,' said Jay. 'I mean no offence, but Ves and I have angered no one.'

'Yet,' I muttered.

Jay ignored that. 'If we request a tour, as representatives of the Society, surely they would agree?'

'Of course they would,' said Mabyn.

'Great.'

Her lips quirked in a sardonic smile. 'Anything remotely objectionable is well hidden, and believe me, you won't find it without help.' She held up a hand as Jay opened his mouth, forestalling his words. 'I cannot help you there. Forty years, remember? I am out of touch with their present arrangements.'

'Not to worry,' I said. 'I have a plan.'

Jay eyed me warily. 'Is it by chance a Mad Ves Plan?'

'A what?'

'Mad Ves Plans make perfect sense to Ves, but less so to anyone else. They are the result of Ves's unique worldview, combined with a splendid disregard for convention or rule and a degree of blithe recklessness.'

'You don't like my plans?'

'They frighten the life out of me,' said Jay. 'It's therefore galling to have to admit that they sometimes work.'

'Usually,' I corrected.

'All right, usually. So what's the plan?'

'I am going to show them the pup.'

'What? Ves, if they are the ones responsible for breeding that puppy, we'll be in big trouble.'

'I don't think they are. Or *if* they are, they may be unaware that one has got away. They'd be quite interested to hear about that, don't you think?'

'Oh? How do you figure that?'

'Because this place is so reclusive. If this is where the pup came from, how did it end up in a medieval ghost-cottage in East Anglia? If the pup came from here at all, then somebody took it out of Dappledok into England, and that is a circumstance that's likely to be frowned upon by the School. I think they would like to know about it, don't you?'

'Like I said,' said Jay with a sigh. 'Blithe recklessness.'

I looked at Mabyn. 'Would you like to be on better terms with your family again?'

'What,' said Mabyn suspiciously, 'did you have in mind?'

'If, say, you heard about this Goldnose matter and came here out of concern for the school, that might win back a little favour.'

'They would only think I was here to make trouble for them.'

'Which,' Jay put in, 'we very possibly are.'

'Let's just see how it goes, shall we? Anyone who's with me, come along.' I left without waiting for a reply. I knew Jay would follow, and it wasn't especially important whether Mabyn did or not.

I thought for a moment that she would not, but then I heard her uneven footsteps following along behind Jay's — the intermittent *clip* of her one remaining heeled shoe on the stone floor. 'You'll never even find the school without me,' she called.

'Is it that well-hidden?'

'It's more that it's spread all over Dapplehaven by now, and beyond. It had thirteen different buildings last I knew, and that was some time ago. What you'll want is the kennels, which used to be on the north-eastern edge of the town.'

'Lead on,' said Jay with a courtly half-bow.

Mabyn led us all the way back down the stairs again. Her cousin Doryty lingered still in the hall. 'And where are you going?' snapped she when she saw Mabyn.

'To the school.' Mabyn spoke firmly. 'We have come on a matter of some urgency, and I think the school will want to hear of it. Please ask whoever is currently serving as its headmistress to meet us at the kennels.' She did not await a response, but swept out of the front door with her chin held high.

Doryty scowled, but made no move to stop either Jay or I as we went past.

'Headmistress?' Jay wondered. 'It couldn't be a head-master?'

Mabyn did not appear to hear, and marched on up the street oblivious of Jay's question.

So I hauled out our lovely book. 'Mauf. Is the Redclover School at Dapplehaven always led by a headmistress?'

'Typically,' said Mauf. 'Spriggan society tends strongly towards the matriarchal.'

'I knew I liked them,' I said.

THE KENNELS, HAPPILY, HAD not been moved in the last forty years, though judging from Mabyn's reaction they had been altered. She led us down myriad curly streets, past a great many houses and little shops (I wanted to investigate some of the latter, but Jay would not let me). The streets were mostly empty, but we passed a few citizens of Dapplehaven here and there — spriggans, mostly, dressed in such a riot of different clothing styles that I could detect no clear pattern. A society with no prevailing fashions? Unusual. We attracted some attention ourselves; I could well believe that they did not often see a couple of humans wandering down their wonky boulevards.

Just where Dapplehaven's houses thinned and gave way to rocky heathland, there was a cluster of low-roofed buildings arranged around a central courtyard. The sounds of yapping and baying announced the kennels' presence rather before they came into view; they were obviously still in use.

But Mabyn looked around with a frown, apparently nonplussed.

'Something the matter?' said Jay.

'There used to be a lot... more,' said Mabyn. 'Of everything.'

The school had downsized its kennels in recent years, hm? Perhaps things were not going so well for them.

The kennels also appeared oddly deserted, in spite of the noise. We wandered about for a while, peeping into each of the white-walled buildings in turn. There were plenty of beasts there, including a litter of gorhounds just like the one my pup presently resembled, but there were no people.

The pup swiftly proved a handful. Her face had popped up out of the bag the moment the first forlorn yap had reached our ears, and she had ridden like that, ears pricked up and on high alert, until we got within sight of the kennels. After that, nothing would restrain her. I managed to catch her as she swarmed out of the bag, but she writhed like a wild thing in my arms and it was like trying to hold on to a thrashing eel. She bested me with embarrassing ease and hit the floor with a bounce.

Off she went at a run.

She did not seem disposed to go far, so I was not unduly worried. She came back into view from time to time, tearing past with her tail flying behind her, jaws wreathed in a huge puppy grin as she went from kennel to kennel, greeting every single other creature there.

It was the pup who finally found signs of sentient life, in a manner of speaking. I had not seen any sign of her for a few minutes, and Jay and Mabyn and I had gathered into a knot in the central courtyard, deprived of any particular objective for the moment and awaiting the arrival of the headmistress (supposing she chose to answer the summons). The pup suddenly erupted from a nearby kennel, vaulting over the door in a single leap, and dashed towards us, tongue lolling.

The door she had just jumped over slammed open in her wake, and a spriggan came dashing out after her. I could swear we had looked into that same building only a few minutes before, and seen no one, so how we could have missed him I do not know. He came barrelling in our direction, but not because he had the slightest interest in us; all his attention was fixed upon the pup.

He swiftly proved himself an adept handler of puppish creatures, for he stymied all her attempts at evasion, anticipating her movements with remarkable prescience, and intercepted her as she swung around behind Mabyn. He pounced, and scooped, and emerged victorious, with a wriggling and indignant pup captured in his arms.

I took brief note of his posture. Was he holding the pup in some special way? I couldn't see how, but by one means or another, he was holding her fast where I had completely failed.

'I am so sorry,' I said to him, holding out my arms to receive her. 'Lacking your aptitude with such creatures, I could not persuade her to stay with me. She's a little over excited by all the company, I'm afraid.'

The spriggan looked up, as though noticing my presence for the first time. His gaze travelled from me to Jay and then to Mabyn, but he betrayed no sign of understanding what I had said.

Mabyn stepped in, to my relief. She spoke to him in a string of incomprehensible words, presumably repeating what I had said, for she gestured once or twice at me.

But the spriggan shook his head, so emphatically that the flat cap he wore almost fell off. He said something in response, with a vehemence I interpreted as excitement.

He shook the pup slightly as though to say, *look at this!* And I noticed that he was shaking.

Mabyn winced, and turned to Jay and me. 'He asks where you got a Goldnose pup from.'

'He... he can tell she is not a gorhound?'

'He says he would know a Goldnose anywhere, whatever disguise they wore.'

Oh dear. I hoped there were not too many people around who could so easily see through our deception. 'Please tell him that we are here in hopes of discovering an answer to that very question. We do not know where she came from.'

Mabyn relayed this, which seemed to dumbfound the kennel worker. He stood in thought for a moment, a look of total befuddlement on his face. Then, to my mild indignation, he turned around and wandered off in the direction of the kennel he had emerged from.

'Hey, wait a moment,' I said. 'That's our pup.'

'He is fetching her some milk,' said Mabyn. 'He said a moment ago that she's too thin, and he thinks you have not taken good care of her.'

'She's only been with us a few days!' I protested. 'She was starving to death when we found her.'

'That is hardly surprising,' said a new, unpromisingly stern voice from somewhere behind me. 'She needs a special milk, which I do not suppose she has been getting.'

I turned. Behind me stood a woman almost of my own height — a human woman, not a spriggan — and almost of my own age, too, if I judged correctly. She presented an unassuming appearance, with dark hair drawn into a ponytail and discreet make-up. She wore a deep blue trouser suit with a black blouse. On the lapel of her jacket was a tiny silver pin in the shape of a pegasus.

'You must be in charge,' I guessed.

She inclined her head to me. 'My name is Jenifry Redclover. I am the present headmistress of the school.'

Now that I looked more closely at her, I detected traces of something else in her face that might indicate a mixed ancestry. Slightly overlarge eyes, for one, and an unusually wide mouth. Still, it did not make much sense for her to share a surname with Mabyn, who could scarcely be more different.

'It is something of an honorific,' she explained, with a faint, unamused smile. 'To become the manager of this school is to become a Redclover, if you were not one already.' I supposed my puzzlement must have shown, which was clumsy of me.

I hastily changed the subject. 'A pleasure to meet you, Ms. Redclover. May I ask whether the pup came from these kennels?'

'That is quite impossible. To so blatantly flout all Magickal Accords would result in the school's permanent closure. It could never be worth the risk, however valuable the Goldnose may be.'

At this point, Mabyn decided to reassert herself. 'I hope that is the truth,' she said in a brisk tone. 'It has come to the attention of the Hidden Ministry of England, Ireland, Scotland and Wales that the breed has resurfaced against all prohibitions. No good can come to those responsible, and if the school is involved there is a great deal of trouble brewing.'

'Hello, Mabyn,' said Jenifry flatly. 'How good of you to return.'

10

MABYN AND JENIFRY REDCLOVER, the spriggan and the human headmistress, eyed one another with bristling hostility. 'Must you bring threats?' said Jenifry. 'The school has never offered you the smallest harm.'

'I bring warning, not a threat,' said Mabyn, though she looked nonplussed. 'How do you know me? I do not think we have met.'

'Your portrait still hangs in the heritage gallery.'

Mabyn looked pleased. 'I thought they would have taken that down by now.'

Jay coughed. 'You've an official portrait?'

'She is a former headmistress,' said Jenifry. 'That makes her a part of our history, whatever her subsequent choices may have been.'

'I made them for good reason,' said Mabyn.

Jenifry looked unimpressed. 'I am sure you did. At any rate, I must get to the bottom of this.' She straightened her shoulders, and left in the direction of the kennel which had previously swallowed up the man in the flat cap — and our pup.

Mabyn gave a soft sigh. 'I tried to tell Milady I was the wrong person to send.'

'Milady knows what she is doing,' said Jay. 'I am sure she had her reasons.'

I smiled faintly, remembering the early days of my career at the Society, and the unshakeable faith I, too, had enjoyed in Milady. Not that I doubted her now, as such. But however remarkable she may appear, she was as human as the rest of us somewhere behind the disembodied voice. I hoped Jay was right, and that this time she knew what she was doing.

For myself, I pitied Mabyn. Her job required her to take a hard line against the pup, for the Ministry could no more support the widespread return of the Goldnoses to the world than any of its sister organisations did. But she clearly felt some residual loyalty to her former home, and if she was once the headmistress here... she must have been very dedicated.

'I am sure we can contain this issue before it has chance to cause much trouble,' I told her in my most reassuring tone, secretly crossing my fingers in hope that I was to be proved right. 'Only one pup has been found.'

'If it came from here, there are more,' said Mabyn.

I was worried about that possibility, too, though perhaps not for the same reasons. No matter what the laws said, the Goldnoses were innocent of wrongdoing in themselves; it was only in the hands of the wrong person that they had any power to cause harm. Did they not have a right to exist? Was it not our duty to protect and preserve all magickal creatures, as we did with books and artefacts and treasures — even the dangerous ones? A series of laws that had effectively wiped out several entire species did not sit well with me.

This point of view had nothing whatsoever to do with the heart-rending cuteness of the pup, I swear. I was totally detached and objective.

Anyway, I was concerned that more pups were out there somewhere, starving to death as our pup's siblings had done. And they could be anywhere. Anywhere at all. We needed to find the source before any more of them died, and then Jay and I needed to find a way to protect them — with or without Milady's concurrence. I was fairly sure I could successfully argue that case, but Milady sometimes came down hard on the side of the rules. You never could quite tell which way she would go.

Jenifry Redclover shortly returned, the becapped sprig-gan with her. I was relieved to see our pup trotting along at their heels, though a bit less pleased to see that the beast had lost her disguise, and was restored to all her gold-furred splendour.

She came straight up to me, and begged to be picked up. I, of course, was delighted to comply.

Mabyn, Jenifry and the kennel worker watched this dis-play of affection in unreadable silence.

Jenifry spoke. 'Jory is confident that the pup did not come from this school. He also says that it is not — it cannot be — a descendent of the last such beasts that were known to exist before the laws forbidding their procre-ation.'

I blinked. 'What? Why not?'

'Because the horn she bears is out of keeping with that theory. The Goldnose was eventually arrived at through the cross-breeding of a few other species, one of which possessed a horn like the one you see adorning the forehead of your pup. But that feature gradually bred out, and was gone by the time the laws were introduced.'

'So...' I did not know what to say first, so many thoughts were churning in my mind.

'*Is* she a Goldnose?' said Jay.

Jory said something emphatic.

'Yes,' translated Jenifry. 'Her capabilities are not in question. But she is a very early example of the breed.'

'How is that possible?' I gasped.

Jenifry shook her head. 'I do not know. Either someone, somewhere, has been attempting to recreate the species by going back to its beginnings, and starting again from scratch, or... or something far stranger is happening. And I suspect the latter, for according to Jory, most of the creatures who were originally cross-bred to arrive at the Goldnose have been extinct for longer than the Goldnose itself.'

I retrieved the book. 'Mauf,' I said crisply. 'Tell us what you know about the Dappledok pups, otherwise known as the Goldnose species. Everything, please, from the beginning.'

Mauf swelled with importance, almost doubling in size. 'The species commonly known as the Goldnose was primarily the work of one person, a spriggan of the name of Melmidoc Redclover. The idea was conceived in the autumn of 1617, and work swiftly began. The goal was to successfully interbreed a variety of beasts whose collective talents included unusual senses for precious materials of one sort or another, heightened tracking abilities, tenacity, and biddableness. It is noted that the project was completed successfully in a surprisingly short space of time — too short, some said, though no particular theory as to how it was done has ever been presented. Within a few years, the earliest hybrids were being successfully trained to sniff out precious metals and jewels from some distance away.'

'What did these look like?' I said. 'In detail?'

'These earliest of the Goldnoses had pelts of varying colours, and the diminutive "unicorn" horn.'

'But this feature faded over time? The horn?'

'It was felt that the horn was unnecessary, for it served no particular purpose, and it was too distinctive a feature. Subsequent generations were bred selectively to eradicate the horn, though in the process the range of colours was lost, and they became predominantly goldish yellow.'

'By when did that happen?' put in Jay.

'The last recorded instance of a horned Goldnose was noted in 1624.'

Seven years? Within a mere seven years of the project's inception, they were already at the stage of making refinements to an otherwise perfect breed? 'That is far too fast,' I said, puzzled. 'Even if the Goldnoses breed unnaturally quickly, surely that is too fast.'

'Many said so,' agreed Mauf. 'In a letter to her sister in 1621 — subsequently published in a volume entitled, "Diverse Correspondence Between Two Sisters" — the Viscountess of Wroxby observed, "Do you Persist in wishing to bring a Goldnose Pup into your household? I am Persuaded you would never know another moment's peace, being forever deprived of your Jewels &c. And you should consider, that though they may be Fashionable, there is some manner of Mystery surrounding their existence about which I cannot be Easy. I wish you would abandon the notion." Which, by the by, she did.'

'Good to know,' murmured Jay.

Mabyn, who had been trying to find opportunity to speak for a few minutes, now cut in. '*Yes,* that is all very interesting, but what of Melmidoc Redclover? I am certain I have heard that name, but I cannot think how.'

'Melmidoc Redclover was thrice invited to take up the headmastery of the school, but declined, for he preferred to devote all of his time to his various projects. His was the mind behind five of the eight breeds for which the school became famous.'

'Perhaps that is how I have heard of him,' said Mabyn, though she frowned, and her tone was doubtful.

'He is primarily remembered for his disappearances, however,' said Mauf blandly.

'What?' I said.

'*What?*' Mabyn and Jenifry said at the same time.

'Disappearances, plural?' put in Jay.

'He disappeared,' persevered Mauf. 'Repeatedly. Four times were recorded, though there may have been more. The first time was in 1599, at the age of sixteen, when he was but a scholar and had not yet distinguished himself by any particular measure. He was absent for three and a half months, and was either unable or unwilling to give any account of his movements upon his return. He vanished again six years later, for almost a year. His third disappearance came at the more advanced age of forty-three, and lasted only three weeks. And he vanished again, for the fourth and (to my knowledge) final time, in 1630, at the age of forty-seven. He was never seen or heard from again.'

A silence fell which could only be termed Flabbergasted. Yes, with a capital F.

'There is clearly more to this than meets the eye,' said Mabyn.

'I have heard the name,' said Jenifry. 'I have seen him, even. Not in the flesh,' she said hastily, as everyone turned to look at her. 'His portrait. There is a gallery devoted to former headmasters of the school, and some few others whose contributions are considered to be of particular significance. Melmidoc Redclover is one of them. The odd thing is...' She hesitated, a deep frown clouding her brow. 'Your unusually talkative book asserts that he disappeared at the age of forty-seven?'

'So it is written,' said Mauf, somewhat huffily.

'He is, in essence, a library all in one,' offered Jay. 'He has absorbed the entire contents of the library at the Society, and quite a lot of... of other libraries, too.' Perhaps he hesitated to name Farringale just then for fear of derailing the conversation altogether; probably wise of him.

Jenifry gave a faint smile. 'I do not doubt you, for he is obviously a marvellous enchantment. The thing is, this portrait is clearly labelled as Melmidoc Redclover, and judging from the clothes he is wearing, and the style of the painting, it dates indeed from the mid seventeenth century. But... but you see, he is depicted as a rather older man. His hair is entirely grey, his face much more lined than that of a man not yet fifty. I took him to be twenty years above that age, at least.'

Stranger and stranger. 'Could the portrait have been made retrospectively?' I suggested. 'As a commemoration, perhaps, of the man he might have been had he not disappeared?'

'It is possible,' Jenifry conceded. 'But...' she paused again, seeming unsure how to phrase her thoughts. 'It is his expression,' she said. 'The portrait lingered in my memory because it is much more — more *real*, than many of the others. It is not a stiff, staged piece. His face is full of character, and life, and humour. I used to like to look at it. It looks like a portrait taken of a model who was very much alive, and in no way resembles a fading memory of a man who had not been seen for at least twenty years.'

'I cannot imagine, though, why a man would be universally set down as vanished for good if he was not, in fact, gone.'

'Has the painting always hung in that gallery?' asked Jay.

Jenifry blinked. 'I do not know. Mabyn?'

Mabyn slowly shook her head. 'I do not particularly recall it from my day, but that does not mean it was not there. I never did take much of an interest in the gallery.'

'Except for your own portrait,' said Jenifry.

Mabyn took this unabashed. 'Except for that one.'

I called Val. She did not answer, so I left a message for her. 'Val, please find everything you can about one Melmidoc Redclover, of the Redclover school in Dapplehaven. Matter of grave urgency.' I chose not to relay the things we had already learned about him, for they were mightily confusing, and I did not want to influence Val's thinking or cloud her findings.

Next, I called Zareen, who picked up after two rings. 'What's up, Ves?' she said briskly.

'So that mass exorcism you pulled,' I said without preamble. 'I don't suppose it can be undone, can it?'

'You mean can I bring three vaporised ghosts back from oblivion? No.'

'Damnit.'

'Why?'

I filled her in. It took a few minutes. When I had finished, she gave a low whistle. When she spoke, I could hear her grin. 'Nice little mystery you have there. So you were wanting to ask them a few questions?'

'I was. The thing is, Zar, that there is a pattern emerging here. This began with a vanishing house, and now we have a vanishing Redclover on our hands to boot. Coincidence?'

'No such thing as,' she said cheerily.

'Yes there is.'

'Fine, but not often. Tell you what, there's one thing I can do.'

'Anything would be good.'

'I've wondered before about all the places that house was going to. I dug up a few instances of its wandering about near (or in) the town of Bury St. Edmunds, but I never looked beyond — and there are gaps of years between most of those reported sightings. I'll see if I can find out where else it might have been parking itself.'

'Especially around the first half of the seventeenth century,' I said. 'Those were the Melmidoc Redclover years.'

'I'll do my best. Don't get your hopes up too high though, Ves. It wasn't a distinctive cottage, and unless other people saw it literally vanish into the mist, I won't be able to track it.'

'Do what you can,' I said. 'Thanks, Zar.'

I hung up, to find that the rest of my companions had gone into a huddle. Jay looked up as I joined them. 'We have a plan,' he told me, with great solemnity. 'Jenifry is to investigate the portrait. Mabyn is going to "raid" the school and scour its records.'

'Raid?' I echoed, intrigued by the emphasis he had laid on the word.

'The school is a little... private, about its records,' said Jenifry, a little shamefaced. 'Even I have been unable to gain access to everything, and that has occasionally made me curious. Jay thought that Mabyn might be able to make better progress, if she makes a show of authority.'

Mabyn looked as though she would very much enjoy making a show of authority.

'Good idea,' I said. 'And when that fails?'

'When?' Jay looked a bit hurt.

'It is a good idea as a diversion,' I said, as gently as I could. 'But if you get pushy with people, they usually push back. At best, they'll make a show of compliance while secretly opposing you every step of the way. While someone is kindly showing Mabyn around the records room, with a suitable show of deference, someone else will be quietly relabelling, or hiding, or outright removing, anything that isn't judged to be suitable for public consumption.'

Jay frowned. 'What do you suggest, then?'

'Mabyn and Jenifry proceed as planned. Meanwhile, you and I will infiltrate the records room and have a poke around. And if we spot anybody trying to hustle any juicy-looking boxes of papers out of the way, we can intercept them.'

'You just like sneaking around,' said Jay.

'I do, actually. I adore sneaking around.' I beamed at him.

I detected traces of annoyance in Jenifry's face, though I could not guess at the reason why. Mabyn, though, was more amiable. 'I think she is right,' said she, and my heart warmed to her on the spot. 'There is one problem, though.'

'Oh?' I said. 'What's that?'

She was not looking at me. Her gaze was fixed somewhere over my head, at the approximate level of the horizon. 'Archibald,' she said.

I turned, and there indeed was the purple-scaled vision of dragonhood winging its way rapidly towards us. 'But don't you two go way back?' I said, turning back to Mabyn.

'Archibald obeys the orders of one person only, that being the Mayor,' said Mabyn. 'He is usually employed to summon miscreants to an impromptu audience.'

'Is that what happened before?'

'Yes.'

'But you weren't taken to the Mayor, were you?'

She blinked at me. 'I was. That's Cousin Doryty.'

'She's the *Mayor*?' said Jay. 'What was she doing answering the door?'

Mabyn shrugged. 'Dapplehaven is a peaceful place, most of the time. Perhaps she was bored.'

'Or perhaps she was more interested in our presence here than she let on,' I suggested.

'Either way,' sighed Mabyn, 'Archie is here to pick up at least one of us, and that means Doryty's changed her mind about letting us wander off.'

We turned as one to watch the approach of the dragon called Archibald. He gained on us with appalling speed and swooped, claws extended. I tried to convince myself that he was going for Mabyn again, but no. Those claws reached out, glittering bright silver in the sun, and the person they grabbed this time was — *inevitably* — me.

11

And, as it turned out, Jay. Archibald wrapped one set of claws around my shrinking middle, and the other around Jay, and took off with both of us in tow. We watched, helpless, as Mabyn and Jenifry Redclover receded beneath us — and Jory the kennel-keeper, too, with our pup still in his arms.

'Inconvenient,' observed Jay, the word emerging as a squeak.

Archibald's grip was a bit tight, at that. I was feeling breathless myself, and I felt like I had an iron band vice-tight around my ribs. 'Archie,' I called. 'You couldn't squeeze a bit less, by any chance? We are fragile creatures, prone to breakage.'

The dragon expelled a whistle of air through his nostrils, and to my surprise, huffed out a clear *No.*

'Oh,' I said.

'You might fall,' the dragon explained.

'That would make for some serious breakage,' I had to agree.

'Fair,' said Jay. 'But don't squeeze too tight. We ought to arrive alive at the Mayor's, no?'

'The Mayor?' said Archibald. 'Why would you want to see her?'

'That... isn't that where we are going?'

'No...' said Archibald, and something about the way he said the word struck me as a bit shifty.

I patted his leg with the hand that wasn't clinging desperately to my shoulder-bag, and Mauf. 'Where are we going, then?' I asked.

'There is something you should see,' said the dragon.

'Oh?'

A pause. 'I... I heard what you were saying,' said Archibald, and he definitely sounded shame-faced now.

'From *how* far away?' Jay yelped.

'I have very good ears,' said Archibald with dignity.

'And a fair bit of magick, too?' I suggested.

'Well, *anyway,*' said the dragon. 'I used to take Melmidoc places.'

'You knew Melmidoc Redclover?'

'His brother was the longest-running Mayor Dapple-haven has ever had,' said Archibald. 'They were always together, and so... we were always together, too.'

Could a dragon be forlorn? Apparently. 'You miss your friends?' I guessed.

'I do not like Doryty,' said Archibald. 'She is foul-tempered.' His enormous tail thrashed.

'We did not like her very much either,' I said soothingly.

'No one does.'

'Odd, then,' said Jay, 'that she is the Mayor. How did that happen?'

'No one else wanted the job. It is very boring.'

I risked a glance down. Archibald was taking us well away from Dapplehaven, and the ground was rising steeply beneath us. We were, I judged, sailing up the side of a low peak I had briefly glimpsed at some distance from the town. It did not, at least from this angle, look scaleable by any normal means.

'Is this where you used to take Melmidoc?' I asked.

'Melmidoc and Drystan,' said Archibald happily. 'All the time!'

Jay put in, 'Have you taken anybody else there since?'

'Once. The Mayor made me do it. They took away everything that was Melmidoc's, and they made it so I am not allowed to land there.'

'They... how did they do that?' said Jay.

'Oh, there are spikes,' said the dragon cheerfully. 'So I will have to drop you.'

'Onto spikes?!'

'There is a bit that is safe,' said Archibald, with enviable serenity. 'You will not break, because you are smaller than I am.'

'How are we...' I began. I had been going to say, *How are we going to get off the mountain*? For if Archibald could not land there, he could not retrieve us either. But the wind whipped my words away as we began to descend towards a windy, and lamentably cold, hilltop, and since we were, moments later, released from Archibald's claws without warning and flying through the air, there was not much point in finishing the sentence.

It hurt, rather a lot.

'Ouch,' croaked Jay, to my relief, for it proved at least that he was alive.

'Nnngh,' I said, somewhat less coherently. I'd landed on one arm and one hip, both of which smarted painfully, particularly since the ground up there was all highly un-comfy rock. You'd be surprised how little difference a liberal covering of moss and heath make when falling from... any kind of height at all.

I hauled myself, creakily, to my feet. 'Mauf?' I said. 'Still alive?'

'Can I be said to be living?' answered Mauf, in his dry, didactic tone. 'Arguably—'

'Great,' I cut in. 'Let's talk about that later.' I looked around. Archibald had not been exaggerating about the spikes. The ground was covered in them. They were at least a foot long each, they were made of something as hard and bright silver as steel, and they had sharp points. The spot we had landed in was only a few feet across, and an uneven patch in the ground suggested that there might once have been a tree growing there. I wondered whether Archibald had happened to the tree.

'They really didn't want anybody coming up here,' I said.

'But why not?' Jay turned in a circle, surveying the scene. There wasn't much to see. The peak of the hill was not very wide, and it declined steeply on all sides to the ground some way below. We had a fine view over Dappledok Dell, and it made for a glorious vision: rolling dales, vibrant meadows, and the town of Dapplehaven nestled adorably in the middle.

Lovely, but unhelpful. All there seemed to be at the top was a roughly circular space full of spikes.

'Archibald?' I looked up, but he had gone. 'Did he expect this to somehow make sense to us?' I said with a sigh.

Jay looked around again. 'Are we missing something obvious? What's up here?'

'Spikes.'

'All right. Why are there spikes up here?'

'To prevent Archibald from landing.'

'Why?'

'Because he was bringing people like Melmidoc up here, and someone disliked that for... reasons unknown.'

'Those are the obvious answers. What about the less obvious? Maybe these spikes were not aimed at Archibald.'

'How many dragons do you suppose there are in Dappledok? They are not exactly common.'

'It's probably fair to say that most magickal beasts were once a lot more common than they are now,' Jay pointed out. 'But it does not have to be a dragon, does it? I wouldn't think anything could land up here with these in the way.'

I thought about that. 'The ground is quite flat.'

'It is. Unusually flat for the terrain, would you say?'

'I might say that, indeed.'

'And,' said Jay, picking his way through the spikes to the edge of the plateau, 'if some of these bushes and such were to be cleared away, we might discover it to be unusually circular, too.'

'So it's shaped. That suggests that...um.' I hauled Mauf out of the bag again. 'Mauf, do you know anything about this place?'

'No,' said Mauf.

There were, after all, a couple of drawbacks to Mauf the Magick Book. For one thing, he could only know about something if someone had obligingly written it down, and people often did not do that with secrets. For another, there was no getting at what he did know if you didn't come up with the right question.

'Nothing about anything called, say, Dappledok Peak or Mount Dappledok? Something like that?'

'No,' said Mauf again, and then: 'Is that where we are?'

'How about buildings?' said Jay. 'Any lost or unaccounted for—'

'Dapplehaven Tower,' said Mauf.

Jay and I blinked stupidly at each other. 'Um,' I said. 'What?'

'Dapplehaven Tower, occasionally referred to as the Striding Spire. It used to, er, tower over the town of Dapplehaven, if you will excuse the pun, but it was dismantled in 1630.'

'1630! Why was it dismantled?'

'The official reason cited was unstable foundations. There were safety concerns in high winds.'

I jumped up and down a couple of times. 'Would you say there is anything in the world less unstable than solid rock?'

'I would not,' answered Jay.

'Now, why was it called the Striding Spire?' I spoke as calmly as I could, but my heart was racing with excitement in anticipation of Mauf's answer.

'Because it wasn't always observed to stand in the same spot,' said Mauf, confirming all my hopes. 'While it was never described as walking around in any literal sense, it was obviously perambulatory.'

'Melmidoc Redclover disappeared in 1630,' said Jay. 'Do you suppose he walked off with the tower?'

'Or the Striding Spire walked off with him!'

'And for some reason, it never wandered back. So that begs the question: where did the Spire wander off to, and what kept it from returning?'

'Other than the spikes?'

Jay considered them with a raised brow. 'Why would someone want to stop the Spire from striding back?'

'Maybe they disapproved of whatever it was Melmidoc Redclover was doing with it.'

'Melmidoc and Drystan,' corrected Jay. 'Archibald said they were always together, didn't he?'

'And Drystan was a Headmaster.' There was something important to be construed from all of that, but I could not decide what it was. I lifted my chin. 'Archibaaaaald!' I yelled to the sky.

'Dragon likes towers,' observed Jay.

'Seems to.' Archibald reappeared in the sky, winging his way back towards us. 'Archie!' I bellowed. 'Was there a tower here?'

He swooped and grabbed me — but missed Jay. The world lurched and spun crazily as Archibald soared away, banked, turned and dived again towards my hapless partner.

The poor boy stood there, braced for impact, trying manfully not to cringe as the enormous purple dragon bore down on him once again.

A yelp might have escaped him as Archie's claws closed around his chest, but this I cannot confirm.

I, on the other hand, shrieked. There is no other word for it.

'Sometimes it was a tower,' Archibald said as he bore us away from the peak once more. 'I liked that the best, because I could sit at the top. The others were not so comfortable.'

'Others?!' Jay and I said it together, and with emphasis.

'They did not like me to sit on the others,' said the dragon mournfully. 'I was always being sent away. But,' he added in a more considering tone, 'some of them were too small anyway, I did not fit. The tower was the best one.'

'They who?' I said.

'Oh, the people inside.'

I was beginning to feel that Archibald, obliging as he was, lacked something in the way of brain. 'What kind of people were they?' I said, as patiently as I could. 'People like Melmidoc and Drystan?'

'Yes, people like them.'

'Magickal people?'

'People like you,' said Archibald. Then he shook the leg in which he held Jay, not at all to Jay's satisfaction. There was another yelp. 'Some of them were a lot like this one.'

'In what way?' I said, feeling a little desperate. I mean, for *goodness'* sake.

Archie lowered his head to sniff at Jay, his huge nostrils flaring. 'I don't know,' he finally pronounced.

'Waymaster,' Jay yelled despairingly. 'He means Waymasters! Must have been.'

Of course. The Greyers' cottage was perambulatory because it had a dead Waymaster bound into its walls. I hoped that those operating the Striding Spire had not been enslaved ghosts as well, for that promised to cast an entirely different light on the whole Redclover operation. 'Were they... alive?' I asked the dragon.

'Of course they were.' He huffed at my stupidity.

'Jay, when you get amazing enough to haul our entire House around at will, let Milady know! She'll be thrilled.'

The glimpse I caught of Jay's face suggested he felt more nauseated than inspired by the idea. 'That's impossible.'

'It is now, but I suppose it wasn't always.'

'I suddenly feel like a weakling.'

'Utterly feeble,' I agreed. 'Pathetic excuse for a Waymaster.'

'Hey. There are times when you are supposed to *contradict* your friends, Ves.'

'Are there?'

'This was one of those times.'

'Was it?'

I got scowled at. I cannot say it was undeserved.

'By the way, Archie,' I called to the dragon. 'Whereabouts are we going now?'

'Oh. The people you were with are at Doryty's now. Would you not like to go there?'

'That will be fine.'

'I don't have to take you there.'

'No, really. It is a good place to go next.'

'I can take you somewhere else, if you like. Doryty will not like it, but I would not mind.'

'Take us to the Mayor, Archie,' I said firmly. 'Then you will not be in any trouble, and we need to talk to our friends anyway.' I hoped they had put some part of our earlier plan into action, but more likely they were trying to find out what had happened to Jay and me.

'I am always in trouble,' said the dragon gloomily. 'She will not like my taking you to the spikes.'

'She does not have to know about it,' I suggested.

A pause. 'You will not tell her?'

'Never,' I solemnly swore.

'Wouldn't dream of it,' added Jay.

Archibald's long, purple tail swished happily. 'Can I keep you?'

'Uhh. We can't stay all that—'

'Of course you can,' interrupted Jay, with a wink at me. 'You're the best dragon I've ever met.'

Archibald puffed up, much the same way Mauf did when praised. Though perhaps not so literally. 'Would you like to be the Mayor?' he replied. 'It is a boring job, but I would make it interesting! We could fly places, and...' He trailed off, apparently unable to think of anything else fun he and Jay could do when Jay was the Mayor of Dapplehaven.

Jay suppressed a laugh with admirable grace, and said only: 'I'll give it some thought, Archie.'

12

ARCHIE RETURNED US TO the tall building inside which we had previously discovered Mabyn languishing alone, and with only one shoe. She was there again, though this time she had halted in the entrance hall. She had the headmistress with her, and the Mayor.

Doryty, Mayor of Dapplehaven, had acquired a socking great amulet from somewhere. It was huge, and very shiny, and it hung around her neck from a heavy gold chain. It looked vaguely like a chain of office, which I suppose is exactly what it was. She had decided to display her authority.

Mabyn was holding our pup in what was essentially a choke hold. The pup, mesmerised by the Mayor's gleaming jewellery, gave a heartrending whimper of protest, and writhed helplessly in that grip; apparently, the bigger the slab of precious materials on display, the greater the poor pup's lust to, er, acquire it.

Headmistress Jenifry stood, arms folded, lips tight with disdain, while the two spriggans bawled at one another.

'The Ministry has every right to demand access to any and all records belonging to any and all magickal establishments!' Mabyn was saying as we went in. At some volume. 'Dappledok Dell may not be precisely under its direct jurisdiction, but—'

'Exactly!' shouted the Mayor. 'Dappledok Dell, and by extension the Redclover School, answers only to those fae courts to which we have historically pledged fealty, and besides those to the Magickal Council of Dells and Dales, to the Commission for Fae Heritage and History, to—'

'I *know* all that,' hissed Mabyn. 'If you insist upon listing every single one we shall be here all day.'

'The Hidden Ministry would not be on that list!' persevered Mayor Doryty. 'It is an organisation by, and exclusively for, human members of the magickal communities, and Dappledok has always been a strictly spriggan or brownie haven—'

'Oh? And the fact that the current headmistress of your precious school is human is neither here nor there, I suppose?'

'It is irregular,' hissed the Mayor. 'But Ms. Redclover is not entirely without the prerequisite heritage, and—'

'Cousin,' said Jenifry Redclover, from between clenched teeth. 'Our associate from the Hidden Ministry has a point, and you know it. Can you not see, that all this obstinacy only encourages the notion that the school has something to hide?'

'What would it have to hide?' demanded the Mayor. 'We have obeyed every stricture placed upon our work, no matter how it has interfered with the school's mission, and since time immemorial!'

'We?' said Jenifry. 'The school is under *my* mastery, Doryty, not yours. Town business is your affair. School business is mine. We are finished here.' She bestowed a curt nod upon the fuming Mayor of Dapplehaven and turned to the door. 'Oh!' she said, upon seeing Jay and I. 'Excellent. We were most concerned.'

'I can see that,' I said drily.

Mabyn unceremoniously dumped my whimpering pup into my arms, whereupon I was too busy trying to keep hold of her to engage any further in conversation with Jenifry.

Mayor Doryty, meanwhile, was rendered still angrier by the reappearance of Jay and I. 'How did you get back in!' she fumed.

'Oh?' said Jay politely. 'Were we supposed to be thrown out?'

Doryty clenched her fists, as though she would like to express her displeasure by inappropriately physical means. In the end, she merely stalked past Jay into the street, roaring as she went, 'Archi*baaaald!*'

'My "cousin" always opposed my appointment to the headmastery,' observed Jenifry, watching this retreat with a tiny, mirthless smile.

'Who appoints the headmistress, then?' I inquired.

'The school has a board of governors. Doryty is one of them, of course, but she was overruled by the rest.'

'Why does she hate you?'

'Because I'm neither a spriggan, nor a Redclover. It is the only time in the entire history of the school that a headmaster has been drawn from neither stock. It's by her insistence that I ended up having to take the Redclover name.'

'Family matters,' I murmured. 'Always tricky.'

'Time to raid the records,' put in Jay. 'And quickly. We're already late.'

Mabyn paused in dusting pup hair off her suit. 'Where did Archie take you, if he didn't throw you out?'

'Take us to the school, if you will,' said Jay to Mabyn and Jenifry both. 'And we'll fill you in on the way.'

WHICH WE DID, OR rather Jay did, because halfway across town I got a call.

'Twas Valerie. 'Ves,' she said crisply. 'Would you like to tell me why you're asking questions about Melmidoc Redclover?'

'Why, is there a problem?'

'Only a total, and virtually impenetrable, block on all information about him. I've tried everywhere. Regular internet has no hits, the magick net has only a vague reference or two behind a big "classified information" wall, we've turned up nothing much in our own library, and when I tried to call in the Baron he came back with no luck either. What does Mauf say?'

'One or two interesting things, which I shall shortly relay, only I didn't want to prejudice whatever you might find— wait. Did you say *virtually* impenetrable?'

'I did, actually.' Val's tone turned smug. 'I haven't been Queen of the Library for so long for nothing, you know.'

'Val! Did you hack something?'

'Sort of, in the magickal sense. Yes. Aided and abetted by your excellent and obliging Baron, so if we're in trouble later, it's all his fault.'

'Did you tell him that?'

'I did. He twinkled at me. How did that date go, anyway?'

'We're wandering off the point here. What did you two reprehensible sneaks manage to dig up?'

'Nothing concrete, but listen. We couldn't get around the classified information barriers, so we decided to find out why everything about him is classified to begin with. That order came down from somewhere way high in the Ministry, Ves, and it was classified under section-something-I-can't-remember of the Magickal Accords of Someday-or-Other pertaining to forbidden uses of magickal arts.'

'We sort of knew that. It's those beasts. He was the mastermind behind the various Dappledok species that were banned.'

'Yes...' Valerie said thoughtfully. 'But, Ves, they don't classify stuff like that. Those kinds of offences, however unusual, would typically fall under more or less mundane misuse of a magickal beast and he'd have a public record of misdemeanour. In fact, he more or less does, though your Baron had to pull some strings to get hold of it as the Ministry's buried it rather deep.'

'He's not *my* Baron, Val — oh, never mind. Spit it out. What else did you find?'

'Does the name *the Striding Spire* mean anything to you?'

'Why, yes. Yes, it does.'

'Right. That's something else your chap Melmidoc was responsible for, and while quite a lot of people were unhappy with him for those thieving little wretches we call the Dappledok Pups — by the way, there were rumours of a thief operating at Home for about six hours, did you know that? Until this morning, when Miranda found a cache of jewels your adorable little friend had hidden away. If the man had a slew of such creations to his name, I'm wondering why they didn't just lynch him and have done with it.'

'*Val.*'

'Sorry. Anyway, somebody was very seriously unhappy with him about that Spire. But even your Baron's contact at the Ministry couldn't find out why. It's that top secret, Ves.'

'Cool.'

'No. Not cool. You are digging your nose into things a lot of important people would like to keep hidden, and by the way there is an *entire ministry* whose purpose is to keep that kind of stuff nicely buried out of sight.'

'Of non-magicker humans, Val! I don't count!'

'You do. I do. There are some things no one is supposed to know.'

'I will bear it in mind.'

'Or in other words, you are wholly unmoved.'

'Of course I am.' We were approaching a handsome brick building with twisty turrets and big, glittery windows by that time, and since its every architectural feature screamed *prestigious school* to this ex-pupil of a prestigious school, I judged that we had arrived at the Redclover educational establishment's main building. 'I have to go,' I said to Valerie. 'But one thing: Mauf told us Melmidoc Redclover had a fine disappearing act going on, which culminated in his total vanishment somewhere in 1630. He also had a brother, Drystan, who was Mayor of Dapplehaven, and they had a tame dragon at their disposal. And that Spire? It, too, had a habit of going walkabout, hence the name, and they took it down the same year Mel disappeared. Can you call Zar? She's digging into that perambulatory cottage business.'

'On it,' said Valerie, and hung up.

I put away my phone, and sidled up to Jay. 'Top, *top* secret stuff,' I told him, brimming with excitement. 'Even Valerie can't find out much about Melmidoc.'

To my disappointment, Jay's reaction was an instant frown. 'Then should we be investigating it at all? We don't need to know more about Melmidoc Redclover, he's been dead for centuries. We're getting diverted from the main point.'

'What was the main point again?'

'Find out where your pup came from, and how it got into the Greyer cottage?'

'Right! Right. But, Jay, everything has to be related. Don't you see that?'

'No.'

'Striding Spire, cottage that goes walkabout. A supposedly extinct Goldnose pup in one, and its original creator in the other. Coincidence? Surely not!'

'Whether it is or not is beside the point. If we've hit a wall with our investigation, we should send what we've found through to the Ministry and let them deal with it.'

'They are dealing with it. They sent us Mabyn, with whose help we now propose to peruse a stash of records entirely unrelated to the Ministry. To quote Doryty the Angry Mayor, the Hidden Ministry has no jurisdiction over the Redclover School, and therefore, the school can do whatever it wants with its records.'

Jay opened his mouth to object again, judging from the lingering frown.

I put my hand over it. 'Jay! Aren't you curious?'

He nodded, still frowning fiercely.

'You realise Milady hires people like us for Acquisitions precisely because we're curious? And tenacious! And difficult to deter!' I optimistically removed my hand.

'Tautology,' said Jay. 'Difficult to deter is the exact definition of tenacious.'

Or in other words, he withdrew his opposition but would in no way be compelled to say so. 'Milady has our back,' I said, beaming at him. 'The Ministry isn't always right, Jay. That's the hard truth about the job we do. We have occasionally ignored Milady's strictures when the need was great enough, and once in a while we have to ignore the Ministry's, too.'

'Why is the need so great this time?'

'Think about it, Jay. What reasonable explanation can you come up with for this pup's existence?' I was still clutching her furry little body to my chest, though she had quietened down now that the Mayor and her shiny jewellery was no longer in sight.

'None whatsoever,' Jay admitted.

'Exactly. Which means something very strange is going on, and will probably continue to go on. We need to find out if there are more of these beasts somewhere, and save them, and get a few specimens for Miranda so she won't kill us. We need to find out how it was possible, apparently, to pluck this one out of, seemingly, nowhere, and plunk it down in a haunted cottage somewhere in Suffolk. And we need to find out why the spriggan responsible for such remarkable, even if questionable, achievements disappeared, and what any of this has got to do with buildings that jaunt about all over the country.'

'Fine, fine,' Jay sighed. 'Colour me convinced.'

I rewarded him with a peck on the cheek and a sunny smile. 'To quote Valerie in all her wisdom: if we're in trouble later, it's all my fault.'

'Valerie said that?'

'Mostly. She's actually blaming the Baron.'

'Good choice.'

We'd paused outside the front door of the school, and so absorbed in conversation had I been that it only then occurred to me that we had been standing there a while. Mabyn of the Ministry and Headmistress Jenifry stood near the door, wearing identical expressions of disquiet, their faces lifted to the air.

'What's the matter?' I asked.

'You can't smell that?' said Jenifry.

I sniffed, and caught a whiff of something acrid. 'Is... is that smoke?'

'It is,' said Jay grimly. 'And it's coming from inside.'

Jenifry hauled uselessly upon the great stained-glass door. 'It's locked. The school's closed by now.'

'Is there a back entrance?' said Jay, already moving.

'This way.' Jenifry led the way at a run, and we followed, all the way around to the back of the great brick pile.

There was a back door, a humble-looking portal of an-cient oak with heavy, black iron hinges. It was open, which was nice. And there was a small inferno of flames erupting out of it, which was less so.

13

So, the main building of the Redclover School was burning down before our eyes. Nice. Worst thing of all? They were not normal, orange-looking flames. They were bright purple, which meant a magickal fire, the kind that leaves nothing to chance.

Jenifry watched for a moment, her face very grim. 'There are measures in place to deal with a fire,' she said. 'But of course, they're all inside the building.'

'Are there likely to be any people in there?' I said, trying not to imagine what it might be like to be one of them just then.

Thankfully, Jenifry shook her head. 'Nothing goes on in here outside of school hours. Jacoby, our caretaker, evicts anyone still lingering by four o'clock, and closes up the building.'

I checked. It was well after half past four.

'Who do we know who might have an aptitude for purple fire?' said Jay, standing at a safe distance with his arms tightly folded.

'A certain purple dragon?' I hazarded.

'Jenifry,' said Jay. 'The records are all in there?'

She nodded. 'Cellar vaults.'

'Was Mabyn right? Does Archibald only answer to the Mayor?'

'He's meant to, and that's normally the case. He might make an exception if he likes you, but Doryty pretends to know nothing about that.'

'So it was probably Doryty who ordered the fire, but it might not have been?'

'Correct.'

Jay looked up into the sky. So did I, and Jenifry, and Mabyn. 'Archibald!' Jay shouted.

No answer came.

'Damn it,' he sighed.

Jenifry was pacing about, staring fretfully at the fire. 'I can make it rain out here for a while, but of what use is that when the fire is in there?'

'How far from that door are the cellar stairs?' I asked her. 'And is there likely to be a locked door in the way?'

'Not far. You'd go down a short corridor and into the rear hall, the stairs are on the left. Yes, there's a locked door, but I have the key. Not that it matters now.'

'It might. Where are these fire-defence measures you mentioned?'

'In every room. There's a bell to the right of every door.'

'Right then.' I shoved the pup — dozing by then — into Jay's arms and set off. Before anybody could stop me, I dived for the purple-flaming door.

This may seem foolhardy of me, but seriously, one of my top talents is shielding magick. All the more so when I happen to have the marvellously amplifying powers of a major Wand at my disposal, which handily, I did. With my Sunstone beauty in my hand, it was the work of a moment to summon an ethereal ward which enclosed me from head to foot, and it was virtually unbreakable.

It was not a perfect solution, though. Main problem: to be that effective, it is also air tight, and that means there is only so long I can stay inside without suffocating.

So I made it quick.

It was my first time wandering about in a blazing inferno, and despite the unusually attractive colour of the flames, I cannot say that I enjoyed it. The corridor Jenifry had described was a tunnel of fire and smoke, and I could see nothing but roaring, hungry flames. It took some nerve to walk through, watching the fire try desperately to claim me, and trusting to my ward to keep them off me. More heat leaked through than I had anticipated, and by the time I reached the rear hall I was shaking violently with fright and sweating profusely.

First: deal with the fire. I soon found one of the bells, positioned just beside the doorframe where Jenifry had said it would be. It was a shimmering crystal creation, exquisitely pretty, and very fae-looking. When I rang it, a clear, tinkling sound pealed through the hall, but I could barely hear it over the near-deafening roar of the fire. Nothing seemed to happen.

I rang it a second time, just in case, and that was all I had time for. If I was going to carry off the second part of my plan, I had to move.

Stairs on the left. There was a door there, which would soon catch alight; flames were licking at the bottom, and all around the frame. Having palmed Jenifry's key ring as I ran past her (ask me another time when and where I learned that skill), I had the means in hand to unlock it. Unfortunately, I had to reach beyond the ward to touch anything, and my hands were shaking so badly that I almost dropped the keyring three times before I found the right key. The *heat*! I could feel my skin burning as I desperately turned the key in the lock, and almost died of relief when it turned and the door swung open.

I all but fell into the blissfully dark, non-flaming stair-well beyond, and hastened down into the cool of the cellar.

It wouldn't be long before the fire spread, so I worked quickly. I made a light, first, by way of several balls of blue fire (yes, the irony was not lost on me) which I sent to float overhead. They illuminated a spacious, open-plan cellar chamber with plain stone walls, many of them lined with bookcases. A long, low chest-of-drawers with at least a hundred drawers in it took up much of the centre of the room, and a couple of study tables occupied the rest.

All of this I dismissed. Nothing sensitive or secret would be kept anywhere so obvious, or so easily accessed. There would be another, hidden chamber somewhere.

I had no time to conduct a search.

'Mauf!' I hauled the book out of my bag, wondering why I hadn't thought to leave him safely with Jay, but blessing my oversight. 'Quick. Help. According to your vast knowledge of secrets, where's a likely place for a secret room in a cellar underneath the Redclover school?'

I was gabbling, but Mauf got me. 'Is there some reason you did not pose this question to the current head-mistress?'

'Because I am looking for old, long-buried information which she, apparently, is not privy to. Super secret, Mauf. Think back to the age of Melmidoc.' I stopped. 'Wait. Can you just... absorb whatever it is? In that way that you do, with other books?'

'If you leave me down here for a few weeks, perhaps I could,' admitted Mauf. 'Do we have a few weeks?'

'We have a few minutes.'

'Then you'll have to find it the hard way.'

'And quickly.' I suppressed the urge to panic. *This is an archives repository, Ves. You are comfortable with archives. Archives are your friend, even if they are about to be set aflame.*

Deep breaths. Yes.

'Second cellar,' suggested Mauf. 'Down underneath. Trap door.'

'Do you see a trap door? Because I don't!'

'I do not *see* anything, I am a book.'

I had wondered before whether Mauf was aware of his surroundings in the visual sense, and if so, how. But this was not exactly the perfect time to ask. 'Any other ideas?' I said desperately. I was by that time running from bookcase to bookcase, shoving at all the oldest ones in case they should happen to swing or turn or vaporise, but nothing happened. I had closed the door on the fire, but smoke was pouring down the stairs and beginning to fill the room, and it was getting hard to breathe.

Then I heard the door slam open, and heavy footsteps thudded down the stairs. 'Ves!'

'Jay? You freaking idiot, what are you *doing?*' He had a ward up, but it was shaky, and already falling apart. This had not, apparently, deterred him from plunging into a burning building.

'What am *I* doing? What are *you* doing?!' Jay bellowed back. 'You are completely bloody insane, and we have thirty seconds to get out of here.'

I extended my superior shield to cover both of us, not that it would help us for much longer. 'But I don't have—'

'Forget it! It's not here.'

'*What?*'

'How about we run first, talk later?'

I might have been willing to risk my own hide for another shot at those papers, but not Jay's. I let him bundle me back up the stairs, Mauf clutched in my left hand and the Sunstone Wand in my right. We almost got lost in the hall, for it was solid smoke by then and we could hardly see. The noise of crackling flames was monstrous, and even my ward began to falter; heat blazed through and began to burn.

But Jay and his sense of direction got us out somehow. We emerged, coughing, into the blissful sunshine of late afternoon, and fresh, clear air had never felt so exquisite. We ran a long way from the door before we stopped, gasping and choking. I was shaking violently. So was Jay.

'Idiot,' I finally told him, when I had recovered breath enough. 'You could have been killed.'

'So could you!'

'I was about to come back!'

'That's a total lie. You were on the opposite side of the cellar to the door, fumbling with a bloody bookcase. You had that foolhardy scholarly zeal going on, didn't you?'

'If you are referring to my academic fervour,' I said imperiously, 'take my advice, and don't ever tell Val you gave it so dismissive a name.'

'Valerie's dedication could never be called into question, but even she would not be fool enough to get herself burned to a crisp in the pursuit of a piece of paper!'

'Are you calling me a fool?' I demanded.

'Yes!'

I found that I had no immediate response to so emphatic a declaration, for he... had a point. 'It was an important piece of paper,' I said in my defence.

'Nothing is that important. And, as I was trying to tell you, what we are looking for probably wasn't in there anyway.'

'Then why has somebody burned the bloody building?' I said, about ready to burst with frustration.

'Maybe they were poorly informed. If it was Doryty the Mayor, well, I am not sure anyone would accuse her of being quite the brightest spark. I'm beginning to think they give that job to the village idiot just to keep them quiet.' Jay suddenly swept me up in a hug, the kind that makes your bones creak. My response was little better than a surprised squeak, and he had squished out all the air I might have used to speak, so I just hung there.

'Your hair is burned,' said Jay in my ear, and let me go.

'*What.*' I checked. He was right. 'Damn it.'

'A fair sacrifice to make for a book?' said Jay, straight-faced.

'Always. Speaking of which...' I put the Wand away and turned my attention to Mauf. 'You okay in there, Maufie?'

'That would be Mauf*ry*,' said Mauf.

'I know how the word goes, I was just — never mind. Glad to see you're unscathed.' I put him away, ignoring his protests. 'So, then,' I said to Jay. 'Where are these super-secret papers, if not in there? Oh, hang on.' I went over to Jenifry, who was pacing about, arms wrapped around her waist, her face turned to the beautiful burning building. 'Those bells,' I said. 'I hit them a few times, but... it doesn't look like they are working.'

She stared at me. 'Then someone has deactivated them.'

'Yes,' I said pleasantly. 'I wonder who it could possibly have been?'

Jenifry's cool composure was unimpaired. 'What do you mean?'

I meant that, as headmistress, Jenifry had the knowledge, the means and the access to everything she would need in order to pull off this little manoeuvre. She knew what the fire defences were, where they were, how they worked, and how to disrupt them. She knew when the building closed, and therefore, when it was safe to set a fire intended only to destroy documents. And she had notably failed to make any efforts whatsoever to bring in help, ostensibly relying on the fire defences to render that unnecessary.

I had slightly mistrusted her apparent helpfulness before, for I had expected some reticence; some challenge to our authority, some attempt to defend the rights of the school. I was now disposed to see it as highly suspicious, but there was not time to have that conversation with her just then. 'You know what I mean,' I told her. 'Luckily, no one died. Why don't you deal with this, and we'll go deal with the other thing somewhere else?'

She began to say something, but I turned my back on her and re-joined Jay.

'I think she has us beaten when it comes to diversions,' I commented.

'Hands down, no contest.' He grimaced. 'Good to know that the old diversion trick works so well.'

'So. Where do you suppose the papers really are?'

'Yes. If the headmistress of this school is willing to destroy her own buildings to keep us away from those papers, don't you think we ought—'

'No.'

That won me a flat stare. 'Is that it? No?'

'We've had this conversation.'

He sighed. 'Fine. Mabyn?'

I had almost forgotten Mabyn, for she had hung back in silence ever since we had emerged from the school building, and had excelled so well at being unobtrusive that I had looked straight past her. But now she stepped forward, visibly gathering resolve, and nodded to me. 'Courageous,' she said.

'Thank you.'

Jay rolled his eyes, but mercifully held his peace.

'When I was headmistress,' began Mabyn, and paused to hand the pup back into my arms. I was welcomed with a lick to my chin, which was nice, though the pup immediately sneezed, which was less so. 'There was…' She stopped, and sighed, and said in a stony voice: 'The reason I am so despised in Dapplehaven is as follows. The post of headmistress of the Redclover School is the highest possible post of authority in this town. The Mayor is barely more than a figurehead, or a distraction. As headmistress, you possess the fullest powers and authority, and access to absolutely everything. You are also bound to lifetime secrecy.

In abandoning my post, deserting the town and, as they see it, joining the opposition, I broke a great many sacred promises. And now, perhaps I must break more.' She took a deep breath, and cast an eye over the retreating figure of Jenifry "Redclover" — who had, apparently, decided at last to do something about the fire. 'The head teacher's quarters are deceptive. The house — Jenifry's house at present, I suppose — looks to be naught but a cottage, but it is much more than that. Anything troublesome, sensitive, especially powerful or dangerous is likely to be kept there.'

'How do we get in?' I said promptly.

'Only the present incumbent of the post can get in.'

'A previous one could not?'

Mabyn's lips flattened into a thin line. 'I doubt it.'

'Can we try?'

Poor Mabyn gave me the helpless look of a woman who is trapped, and knows it. 'We can try,' she conceded. 'But what about Jenifry? She will be on the watch for exactly such an attempt.'

And she would, too, knowing that her fiery diversion was no longer holding us.

Happily, an answer presented itself at that very moment. 'Hello,' came a hopeful voice from some way over our heads. 'Did you need anything burning? I have some fire left. It's purple.'

Archibald descended from above. He did indeed have some fire left; it wreathed his gigantic, scaled body in a crackling shroud, pouring white smoke. We all backed hastily away.

'Archie,' I greeted him warmly. 'Did Jenifry make you burn things?'

'Oh, no!' he said, shocked. 'She would never make me do anything.'

'No?' I said, surprised and dismayed, for that made mincemeat of our neat and tidy theory.

'She's my friend.'

Jay's eyes narrowed. 'Did she ask you to burn things.'

'Yes,' said the dragon, his wings drooping. 'And she promised me a treat afterwards, but there has not been anything.'

I sighed inwardly. Did the portrait of Melmidoc really exist, or had Jenifry fabricated that little mystery in hope of distracting us?

'Would you say *we* are your friends?' I said.

'Yes. Especially that one.' Archie pointed the tip of his fiery tail at Jay, who took an involuntary step back. 'Are you the Mayor yet?'

Jay blinked. 'Ah, no. But we could pretend, if you like?'

Archie gave a wide dragon smile, flashing pearly fangs. 'I like games.'

'I thought you might.'

So, we set fire to Dapplehaven.

14

ALL RIGHT, WE DIDN'T set fire to all of it. Not even very much of it. But enough to keep Headmistress Jenifry very busy indeed, and the Mayor, too. It caused a great deal of frustration, I believe. Jenifry knew what we were up to, and we knew that she knew, but she was in charge here. She could hardly leave her precious town to burn, and its people with it, while she protected her own home. That kind of thing never does a person's public reputation any good, now does it?

We'd chosen empty buildings in disparate parts of the town. Being conscientious, heritage-preserving citizens of the world, we had also selected buildings of little value, material or otherwise, and preferably those with easy access to a body of water besides. And considering Jenifry's professed talent for calling down rain, little real damage would be done, all told. That said, I privately resolved to leave out those details when I made my report to Milady. Why bother her with trifles?

Archibald performed his part with gusto. By the time we had finished, his cloak of purple flame had diminished significantly, and we were no longer in danger of being fried alive if we got too close to him.

Which was convenient, because it was time and past for us to hightail it out of there, and over to Jenifry's cottage. Or whatever it really was.

Archibald was happy to oblige.

'Wait!' I cried, as he reached one vast foot towards me, his claws still crackling with flame. 'You still have too much fire, Archie. We will burn.'

'Oh.' He regarded his foot in pensive silence for a moment, and I felt a twinge of apprehension. What unpromising mental processes might I have sparked in that dim brain of his?

We were in a meadow on the edge of Dapplehaven at the time. A half-ruined barn of ragged oak planks was situated a ways to our left, purple flames licking up the empty frame of its doorway. If there had ever been a farmhouse that went with it, that building was long gone.

Archibald turned his head, coughed, and belched a gout of weak lavender fire all over the grass.

The grass promptly caught alight.

'There,' said the dragon, inspecting his polished claws with greater satisfaction.

The fire roared up towards my feet. 'Er, time to go!'

Oof. Archibald swept me up, then Jay. Mabyn he caught in one back foot, almost as an afterthought as he rose into the skies. I heard her distant squawk of protest, and silently sympathised.

Archibald's getaway was not quite so speedy as I had hoped, for he paused, circling the air, to admire his hand-iwork. The ground below was rather more ablaze than I had bargained for.

'Note to ourselves,' said Jay, eyeing our retaliatory diversion with dismay. 'Be careful when playing with dragons.'

'I would not hurt you,' said Archibald, in an injured tone.

Jay patted his leg comfortingly. 'I know you would not.'

Archibald smiled, and puffed a jaunty little ball of fire into the air.

'At least, not deliberately,' Jay amended, as Archie's fire-ball missed his head by inches.

Mercifully, Archibald flew on after that.

The house of the headmistress proved to be a hum-ble-looking place, though it was amply provided with a large garden ringing the cottage all around. Tim-ber-framed, white-washed and crooked, with a neatly thatched roof, it was spriggan-sized, which must cause Jenifry no end of inconvenience.

It was not, of course, unattended. Archibald landed in the middle of the stone-cobbled street outside of it, but he had trouble squashing his huge bulk even into the widest part of the thoroughfare, and a sweep of his wings upset a cart full of fruit an outraged spriggan was trying to hawk on the corner.

'Jay,' I said, when my adorable and well-meaning partner began picking up spilled produce. 'Focus. Urgent task at hand.'

He smiled sheepishly, handed off the fruit he had collected to the stall holder (who cursed him roundly for his efforts, and tried to box his ears), and re-joined me. Mabyn was already halfway up the street, striding towards Jenifry's cottage with her Minister demeanour firmly in place. Brisk of step, chin high, she swept towards the two guards stationed outside of the front door, looking formidable indeed.

Jay and I hastened to catch up, leaving Archibald to reason with the stallholder.

'I request access,' Mabyn was saying when we reached the house. 'As a former headmistress of Redclover School, and on behalf of the Hidden Ministry, who has reason to suspect—'

'Nobody goes in,' said one of the guards, a relatively beefy-looking spriggan with a domed, shinily bald head and a fine purple uniform. 'Ms. Redclover's orders.'

'*I* am Ms. Redclover,' said Mabyn impatiently.

I was beginning to think that half the citizens of Dapplehaven were called Redclover, and perhaps they really were, for the guards looked most unimpressed.

'We were told that somebody might make an attempt,' said the second guard, a near perfect match for the first, save that he had a full head of dark hair scrupulously coiffed. He looked us over, his leathery face cold. 'If you persist, we are instructed to arrest you at once.'

'You cannot arrest me!' spluttered Mabyn. 'As a representative of the Hidden Ministry, I am immune to all—'

'Ms. Redclover said to make special effort to repel any Ministry folk,' interrupted Guard the First. 'You are immune to nothing, and I suggest you leave at once.'

Mabyn was slow on the uptake and continued to argue. Jay and I exchanged a thoughtful look.

'Usual trick, then?' said Jay.

'I'm thinking so.' I rooted in my heavy and ever-present bag — I will have the right shoulder of a wrestler, at this rate — for my usual supplies, though it took me a moment to find them around the soft, sleeping bulk of Pup and the angled, leather-clad shape of Mauf. I really ought to organise my things a bit better.

But I found them. Two of Orlando's best sleep-pearls, each about an inch across, and encased in a jellyish coating. I gave one to Jay.

I'd retrieved my Wand, too. I threw my pearl up in the air, zapped it with a wave of the Wand, and it burst in a shower of pearly rain all over the nearest guard.

Jay threw his, and I zapped that too.

'Hey—' said Guard the First, as he fell sideways into the road.

Guard the Second followed suit, without uttering so much as a syllable.

They lay there, charmingly inert, and snoring repulsively.

'That shouldn't keep working so well,' Jay said, stepping over the nearest guard.

'Maybe I need a new signature trick,' I agreed. 'You know, the last time I tried to re-order a batch, I got an interrogation from Enchantments? They thought I might be putting them to some manner of misuse.' I reached the door, and tried it. Locked. 'Any keys on those gents?'

'What kind of misuse?' said Jay, bending down to pat the guards' pockets. He shook his head.

'They asked the usual kinds of questions. Was I experiencing any excess pressure at work, that I had been unwilling to report? Was I feeling any strain? When had I last taken time off?'

Jay shook his head at me: no keys. 'People use them to self-medicate?' he said incredulously.

I shook my head back at him, but in my case it indicated despair. 'You are so very new, aren't you?'

Mabyn gave a vast, noisy yawn, and toppled slowly into the street.

'Oops,' I said, regarding her recumbent and deeply asleep form with a twinge of guilt. 'I hoped she wouldn't get caught in it.'

'She could probably use a nap,' said Jay. 'Seems stressed.'

Jay and I quickly moved all three of our victims, the intended and the unintended, to the edge of the street, out of the way of any passing dangers.

'Time for the big guns,' I said, and dived back into my bag. I had a lot of bits and pieces in there, rattling around in the bottom. Not quite as many as usual, since Ornelle, Keeper of Stores, had lately made me hand back virtually everything I'd had on loan (joy-killer extraordinaire). But Orlando's people keep me well-supplied with consumables, and I had a really juicy one in there.

Somewhere.

'Ah!' I crowed, and from the depths of the Receptacle of Everything I produced a stick of bubble gum.

Jay looked at me. He had That Face again. 'Gum? Really?'

'It looks like gum.' I unwrapped it, softened it in my fingers for a moment, then stuck it to the front door of Jenifry's house. 'But you really do not want to eat it.'

I waited.

It began to crackle after a moment, and then it melted into a trickling slime which dripped slowly down the door, taking the wood with it. All of it. Fine old oak planks dissolved into slush and dribbled away, leaving the doorframe nicely empty.

'Don't ever let me eat one of those by mistake,' Jay said as he followed me inside.

'You won't. They taste like poo, and I mean that more or less literally. Safety measure.'

Jay made a gagging noise.

Jenifry had not left it to her guards and her locked door alone to keep us out, of course, but I was ready for that. I flicked the Sunstone Wand as we walked in, surrounding us both in one of my best wards. When the magickal alarm flared, sending waves of searing purple light flooding the interior of the cottage, the surge of power bounced harmlessly off our shared shield, making my ears ring but causing no lasting harm.

'What is it with purple around here?' I muttered.

'You love purple.'

'Exactly. It's *my* signature colour.'

'At least it proposes to be pretty while it fries us to a crisp,' said Jay. 'That has to count for something.'

'My room defences have rainbow fire,' I said proudly.

'Really?'

'No. But not for lack of trying.'

'Is it purple?'

'... Yes. Yes, it is.'

The cottage, as Mabyn had warned us, appeared to be just that: a modest abode, with only a few rooms, and everything in them of the most mundane. Jenifry had a small living room equipped with a worn green velvet sofa and matching chairs, and an array of suitable books. Her kitchen was charmingly old-fashioned, and she had a bedroom at the back.

That was it.

It took Jay and I less than five minutes to explore all this, and we met back in the little hallway, wearing, I imagine, identical expressions of frustration.

'No signs of any secret doorways, I suppose?' I said.

'Nothing so promising. You didn't run into any hidden staircases or trapdoors?'

'Nope.'

It occurred to me to wish that we had asked Mabyn for more detail, though in fairness I imagine every inhabitant of the cottage has their own ways of concealing the secret spaces. Would Mabyn's information have been of any use?

It might at least have been a place to start. Now we had nothing, and Mabyn lay outside in the street, asleep. She would remain so for at least an hour.

My bag rustled, and the pup poked up its head, sniffing the air. I patted her. 'Sweet pup, I wish you could help, but I do not suppose there is anything around here that might interest—' I stopped, because she was writhing like a mad thing to be let down, and succeeded in falling out of the bag altogether before I could catch her. She landed with a snort, but she was up again in seconds, her enormous nose drawing in great gulps of air.

That nose adhered itself to the floor, and off she went, tail high and wagging with excitement.

She went into the kitchen.

'Right, then,' said Jay, and we followed.

But when we reached the kitchen, the pup was not there.

I went back out into the hallway, in case she had sneaked past us somehow, but she was not there, either.

'Huh,' I said.

Jay joined me, and stood regarding the doorway thoughtfully. 'She didn't go straight through, did she?'

'She was circling a bit, but she was following a scent of some kind, so that would account for it.'

'It might.' Jay approached the door again. Rather than walking in a straight line into the kitchen, he did as the pup had done: circled his way over the threshold in an arc, turning a full circle before he went through.

He still ended up in the kitchen, but that had given me an idea.

'I think she went the other way about,' I told him, and stepped forward to try it. 'And with these kinds of things, it is nearly always widdershins that—'

'—does the job,' I finished, after a pause, for my own anti-clockwise circle had landed me in another room, but it was not the kitchen, and there was no Jay.

There was, however, the pup.

15

'GOOD JOB, PUPPY,' I whispered, awed.

For this room was larger than the rest of the cottage put together, and it was packed full. It looked like it might once have been a barn, or something of the like, for it consisted of a large open space with a high ceiling supported by thick, crooked beams, and the windows were near the top of the walls. Shelves, chests of drawers and bookcases were everywhere in evidence, to the pup's delight, for many of them bore objects of obvious value: jewellery, Wands, trinkets and Curiosities, even one or two genuine Treasures as far as I could tell. There were a great many books as well, and — to my relief — a section which was clearly designated for the storage of papers.

I made straight for that, and by the time Jay found his way through the sneaky enchantment on Jenifry's kitchen door, I was up to my eyeballs in crumbling old documents. Figuratively speaking.

'Soooo,' said Jay with a low whistle, walking up behind me. 'Do you suppose all this is legally held?'

'Probably not, considering how eager they've been to hide it. Help me with this, Jay?' I had found a set of four bookcases fitted edge-to-edge and back-to-back, and their shelves were stuffed with old books, proper scrolls with ribbon bindings, notebooks, journals, and everything of that sort. There was so much of it, and we did not have much time before Jenifry would appear — or send someone else to intercept us.

Jay took a look at the job that lay before us, and blanched. 'Try Mauf,' he suggested.

'He says he needs time to absorb this much information.'

'We don't need him to absorb it all, but he may be able to identify what we need.'

So I extracted Mauf. 'Dearest book, if you can contrive to find out whether any of these books and such were written by, or predominantly about, the brothers Melmidoc and Drystan Redclover, our gratitude would know no bounds.'

'I cannot do much with gratitude,' remarked Mauf. 'Do you have something more concrete?'

'What did you have in mind?'

'I want a proper ribbon bookmark. Silk, not polyester. And a sleeping bag.'

'A sleeping— never mind. I will get you anything you like, as long as you're quick.'

'Bookcase to your left,' instructed Mauf. 'Second shelf from the top, third book from the end. Melmidoc's journal of his discoveries, covering the years 1618 to 1630. Bookcase behind that, bottom shelf, a small notebook with crumbling pages — *how* embarrassing — entitled "A Mayor's Recollections of Service," written by Drystan Redclover.'

We hurriedly collected both.

I took the liberty of kissing Mauf's front cover soundly. 'Best book ever.'

The book gave what sounded like a cough, if the rustling of dry pages could ever be termed such. 'That spire you were asking me about. Is that also of interest?'

'Yes!'

'Scroll, bottom shelf. The one with the sumptuous tassels. "An Account of the Deliberations of the Dappledok Council Regarding the Matter of the Spire." I advise you to take all three in that pile.'

I gave him another kiss. 'I love you,' I said as I stuffed him back in the bag.

His response was too muffled to be understood.

I put the books and scrolls in on top of him, trusting that he would enjoy the company sufficiently to forgive me the indignity.

'Time to go,' I told Jay.

He cast a brief, agonised look at the contents of that building, and I could hardly blame him, for I, too, desperately wanted to explore. But he did not argue, perhaps because there came a kerfuffle from the doorway at just that moment, and a voice called belligerently: 'You are trespassing upon private property, and are hereby arrested on the orders of the Mayor!'

Interestingly, whoever it was did not burst straight in, as might be expected. 'I think they are afraid of us,' I remarked.

'Maybe it was the pile of unconscious bodies outside the front door that did it,' mused Jay.

'Could be that. Can you levitate?'

'Badly.' He looked up at the distant windows, and sighed. 'You're thinking of those, aren't you?'

'I am afraid so.' I looked around in irritation, for while there was no shortage of storage spaces, and even a desk against the far wall, there was not a single chair in sight. So much for flying.

'Come on in!' I trilled. 'We give ourselves up!'

On which note, I grasped Jay's hand and shot up into the air, dragging him with me.

I cannot say it was our most successful effort ever. We made it about four feet before we began to wobble, and promptly sank halfway back down again.

Our assailants found their courage and came striding through the door, looking warily about. They were guards like the two we had felled, wearing the same uniforms, though these were equipped with proper Wands: a Jade, and by the looks of it an Opal.

These they levelled at us. 'Stop where you are,' commanded one.

Well, we tried. Hovering for long in mid-air is a talent neither of us possesses, however, so we drifted inexorably back floorwards again. 'Sorry,' I giggled.

The pup trotted over to me, grinning a canine grin, her tail wagging exuberantly. She had an amethyst Wand in her mouth, which she presented to me with great pride.

'Oh, thank you!' I said, accepting it with alacrity. I gave her a luxurious pat, for what a clever, good pup she was!

A guard took it off me moments later.

'That was a gift,' I said indignantly.

'It is stolen property. What else have you taken?'

I rolled my eyes, and sighed. 'Fine, fine.' I unpacked the bag again, offloading all our acquisitions into the wrinkled palms of the belligerent guard.

'Any more?' he prompted when I had finished. 'You will submit to a search.'

Jay did so quiescently enough, but I was not feeling so docile, for if they found Mauf, were they going to believe that the book belonged to me, and not to Jenifry? So as they searched Jay, I cast about for an alternative solution. Sadly, I couldn't get at my brilliant sleep pearls without attracting notice, and I was not perfectly certain that I had any left, anyway.

'I suppose it doesn't have to be a chair,' I said, and kicked over the nearest bookcase. It took a couple of attempts, for it was heavy oak, but it toppled with a nice *bang*, and all its books fell off onto the floor. I felt a pang of guilt over that, for many of them were old and fragile. But needs must.

The other guard had more of his wits about him than I was hoping. He flicked his Opal Wand at me, and succeeded in paralysing my every muscle. I fought, but to no avail; I could barely breathe.

Then the pup sank her teeth into his ankle, making him screech in a fashion I found most satisfying. She followed that up with an athletic jump, closed her slightly bloody jaws around his Wand, and cheerfully pinched it from him.

The paralysis eased.

'Right,' I said. 'We're going.' I bent to scoop up the pup, Wand and all, and at the same time persuaded the nice, empty bookcase that it was feeling energetic. Jay took care of the guard who had hold of him with a solid punch to the face, and jumped onto the bookcase with me.

Up we went.

'The books!' Jay cried.

'Never mind. Mauf's got it.'

'I hope so.'

'Me too. Hup.' I didn't bother opening the nearest window, for the guards were still down there, and one of them still wielded a Wand. So I smashed it, and sent Jay through first.

'Woah,' he gasped as he clambered out. 'Careful, Ves.'

'It's not that far up.' I accepted his help, however, letting him pull me through the window and out onto the roof.

I was immediately obliged to retract my statement, for the ground yawned a long way below; plenty far enough for a mere Ves to go fatally squish, should she fall.

I hung onto Jay. 'Unexpected,' I remarked.

'Any idea where we are?' Jay asked, and that was a fair question, for I had not quite grasped that the view was wholly unfamiliar, and also notably lacking in a town. We were up somewhere high, a clifftop perhaps, and a green valley lay below us, with a pearly lagoon cutting into one side of it. In Dapplehaven we emphatically were not.

My phone rang.

Jay took the squirming pup off me, at some peril to his life, and promptly sat down on the roof. Said roof was also incongruous, by the by, for it was not a barn roof. It was instead rounded, with a peak in the middle, and covered in slate pieces. Also, the window we had climbed through was gone.

I dug out my phone. 'Val,' I said, perhaps a bit shakily. 'This is a bad time.'

'Is your life in imminent danger?' said she crisply.

I tested my footing. Reasonably sound. I followed Jay's example and sat on my haunches, and felt a bit better. 'Probably not.'

'Probably?'

'I mean, we're stuck on a roof with no way to get down, but we probably won't die just yet.'

'Great. Because this is important.'

Another voice cut in: Zareen's. 'Ves, this is *way* important. That cottage? The Greyer place?'

'I remember it,' I said drily.

'Right, listen. I've tracked it everywhere I can, and I admit that it is hard to do, because of its sheer mundanity — nondescript to say the least, right? — but still. Vanishing buildings tend to attract notice, but this one has only done so patchily. In the, what, five hundred years since it began to go walkabout, there have been only a handful of recorded sightings of any vanishing building of its general description. It might have been quietly camouflaged in some unremarkable spot for a lot of that time, sure, but — get this, Ves — I did find one or two other recorded sightings of just such a cottage.'

'And?' I said, not following at all.

'They date from *before* 1508.'

My thoughts spun. '1508, wasn't that the year that Maud Greyer—'

'Killed John Wester and stuffed him into the walls. Yes.'

'But if Waymaster Wester was the one moving the cottage about, how could it have been moving around before that year? Are you sure it was the same place?'

'It's impossible to be entirely sure, but how many late medieval timber-framed dwellings do you know of that had a habit of wandering about?'

'There could have been more. Waymasters were more common, once.'

'They were. And it could be a different building that was spotted mid-vanishment near Colchester in 1432, or that was seen to appear out of nowhere near Ipswich in 1398. But Ves, there's more.'

My hands were getting cold, way up high as we were, for the wind was chilly and it was growing late in the day. I gripped the phone tighter, hugged my bag closer to myself, and said as patiently as I could: 'Go on.'

Val came back on. 'I've been looking into that Spire. Did you manage to find the papers you were after?'

'Yes, but haven't had chance to look at them yet.'

'Right. No tower-like building has ever been sighted moving around Britain the way the Greyer's cottage did, and I think a place like that would attract some notice, wouldn't you? So I went looking for any such reports from Dells or Enclaves or other magickal communities, and bingo. There are a few such cases. Did you get any description of the Spire, by chance?'

'No. My source was a dragon of little brain, who is weak on things like details.'

'There was a tower that used to appear in the heart of the Meyvale Dell, a predominantly sylph community, in the fifteen hundreds. It was said to be all white, but it shone blue at twilight. What does that sound like to you?'

'Starstone, but that wasn't developed into a building material until the early 1600s, so it can't be.'

'Another such tower was spotted twice on the edges of the Barraby Troll Enclave, early 1500s. And there are more such examples, Ves, going back another three centuries.'

My head spun. 'It can't have been starstone.'

'Ves. Get off that roof and go through those papers. I need you to find out whether the tower your Dappledok folk called the Striding Spire was built out of starstone, which would have been brand new and exciting at the time.'

'But—' I stopped, confused. 'But Val, it can't have been starstone.'

'Just find out, Ves. Stop overthinking it.'

I wanted to remonstrate with her some more, but she hung up on me.

Damnit.

I looked at Jay, but before I had chance to relay what Valerie and Zareen had said, he simply gave me a meaningful look and pointed down over the edge of the roof.

I inched my way thither, and peeped.

Below us stretched a tall, slender tower made from blocks of bright white stone tinged faintly with blue — a blue that would flare to brilliance when the sun went down.

I called Val back. 'Val? I think we've found the Spire.'

16

'YOU'VE FOUND THE *SPIRE*?' echoed Val in disbelief. 'The actual building itself?'

'The actual one.'

'Where is it?'

'I don't know, but we are sitting on it.'

'...that's the roof you're stuck on?'

'Right.'

'And you don't know where you are?'

I told her about the cottage, and the secret barn, and the window we had climbed out of. 'I cannot tell if we are in Dappledok Dell anymore,' I concluded. 'I see a valley below with a lagoon in it, the latter having weird iridescent water, and I don't remember that from the Dell. I've a glimpse of sea, more normal colour. And that's it. No houses, no settlements, no sign of habitation whatsoever.'

'Can you get down?'

'No. Not without calling Adeline, and for one thing I am not sure she could make it to wherever we are. For another, I don't fancy trying to get on her back while she's hovering in mid-air about fifty feet off the ground.'

There was silence for a moment. 'Hang on, Ves,' said Val, and hung up.

I looked at Jay.

'Does this kind of thing happen often?' he asked. He had his knees drawn up to his chest and his jacket wrapped around them. We were both getting cold.

'Predicaments of this exact type, no, but in a more general sense... constantly.'

He nodded thoughtfully. 'There is a window,' he said after a moment. 'I explored a bit while you were talking. It's on the other side, about eight feet down.'

'Open?'

'No. But big enough to climb through.'

That did not really augur much. Setting aside the problem of how to reach the window without falling to our deaths, what would happen if we did? Would it prove to be another window like the ones in the barn, and we'd climb through it only to end up somewhere else? I did not want to lose track of this Spire just yet.

On the other hand, we could not just sit on the roof forever, either.

'Levitate?' I said, without much hope. Our joint performance at that art had not covered either of us in glory earlier on.

Jay looked as dubious as I felt. 'I think we'd die.'

'Chances of it are high.'

'If I die without saying goodbye to Indira, she'll kill me.'

'A fate worse than mere ordinary death by falling off a building, no doubt.'

'Much worse.' He looked around, perhaps hoping someone might have left a convenient chair on the roof somewhere. Or a bookcase, we were not picky.

'Did you come across any loose slates while you were daringly risking a plummet to the ground?' I asked him.

He gave me a flat stare. 'You are not witching up a roof tile.'

'I know it's dangerous, but—'

'Dangerous? Have you seen the size of these things?' He selected one to demonstrate with, thus answering my question as to whether or not he had found any loose ones. 'You could barely fit both feet on it,' he said, holding the dark, aged slate up to show me. 'It is windy up here, there is nothing to hold onto, and you would die.'

'There is a building to hold onto!'

'Yes. An extremely tall building, and we are at the top!'

'I just want to use it as a levitation aid. We can inch our way down, stone by stone—'

'How are you still alive?' Jay had folded his arms. It's always a bad sign when he does that.

'Because my ideas are not as crazy as you think, and I have had a lot of practice at slightly foolhardy escapades.'

'Slightly?'

I held out my hands for the slate. 'What if I promise faithfully not to expire?'

He did not hand over the slate, so I set about finding another one.

This prompted a sigh from Jay. 'Ves, I am genuinely worried about this.'

I flashed him a quick smile. 'Me too. But it is going to take Val a while to figure out where we are, if she can at all. In the meantime, we are without food or shelter, and we can hardly sleep up here without falling off. There is only so long we can safely remain aloft, and that means we have to take a risk or two to sort ourselves out.'

With obvious reluctance, Jay passed me his roof tile. 'I am going to thank our lucky stars that your talent for enchanting flying objects is vastly superior to your talent for levitation.'

'Practice, Jay, not luck. Like I said, I've got into trouble before.'

'Do you practice levitation, too?'

'Constantly.'

He grinned at me, though it was a strained expression.

I took up my Sunstone Wand, and set about witching up the slate. The process was much the same, even if the object was rather different, and before long the slate was bobbing buoyantly at my feet.

My pride made it imperative to hide the frisson of panic that shot through me at the prospect of stepping onto it, so I composed my face into a fair impression of serenity, and managed the business as confidently as I could.

Jay sat not far away, hands out, poised to catch me if I somehow managed to fall in his general direction. His face was creased with worry. 'That won't hold your weight,' he said.

'I have reinforced it a bit.' It still felt precarious, though, and Jay had been right about the wind: it buffeted me about atop the too-lightweight tile, and whenever I tried to release my grip on the roof and straighten up, I was almost blown backwards.

So I did it the graceless, undignified way, inching down the roof like a backwards crab, both hands clinging tightly to the tiles within reach. The part where I had to go over the edge was too horrible to recount in any detail. Suffice it to say that the ground yawned far, far below, I absolutely did *not* look down (much), and a great gust of wind caught me halfway through my descent and slammed me against the wall of the tower, almost breaking my fragile levitation aid.

But, I reached the window. Reassuringly big, it was neatly rectangular, and filled in with many small, diamond-shaped panes of glass. It was closed, and locked, and also handsome and old; I did not want to have to employ Rob's trick, and break the whole thing.

So I finagled it. An unlocking charm, amplified by my precious Wand, did the trick; a latch clicked, and to my infinite relief, the central section of the window creaked open.

I shoved it the rest of the way, and all but fell into the room beyond. I received a faceful of dust, first of all, for the floor was thick with it — everything was thick with it. Choking, I drew a fold of my gauzy scarf over my mouth, and held a brief exploration party.

I was not back in the barn, to my relief, nor did I seem to have been transported anywhere else. The room was round-walled, and appeared to be of the right dimensions to fit the tower. Someone had made a comfortable home here, once: a matched pair of elegant, upholstered arm chairs of early seventeenth-century style stood near a stone hearth, with a low table in between. Better yet, an array of bookcases ringed the walls, all stuffed with dust-covered books. I badly wanted to peruse those, of course, but first things first: would one of those chairs fit out of the window...?

It would not, so I chose a stout oak stool which stood near the hearth and enchanted that instead. Within an agreeably short space of time, Jay stood in the tower-top room with me, and without having to brave the same death-defying stunt as I had. The pup, too, was relieved to get her paws on solid ground again, and hopped out of the bag to perform an exploratory circuit of the room, nose to the floor.

Jay still looked shaken, so I gave him a swift hug — and then moved right on to the books.

'Melmidoc's place?' Jay surmised.

'And Drystan both, I'd think, judging from the... chairs...' I lost track of my train of thought somewhere in there, for those books. Those *books!* For a girl with the soul of a librarian, they were like twelve Christmases all in one. Even a cursory inspection soon revealed that they comprised a genuine trove of Treasures, spanning every age from the seventeenth century backwards. My hands shook slightly as I snapped a picture for Val. She would probably faint.

'Ves.' Jay came over, with a book in his hands. He had wiped most of the dust off it, and opened it to the title page. 'What do you make of this?'

It was a genuine illuminated manuscript. That first page was painstakingly inscribed in cramped, but exquisitely neat calligraphic print, the kind that used to take monks an entire day to complete. The text was framed with images inked in gloriously vivid colours, depicting a variety of beasts that were indubitably magickal in nature, though I recognised almost none of them. Were they all extinct?

'I had a leaf through,' said Jay, and took a deep breath. 'Do you see what that says?' And he pointed to a word, prominently placed on the first page, in scrolling hand-writing.

Dramary.

I couldn't breathe.

'Dramary?' I squeaked. 'Is this Dramary's Bestiary?'

Jay just nodded. There weren't words.

See, Dramary's Bestiary is the kind of book people like Miranda cry themselves to sleep over. There are a scant few surviving references to it as one of the most complete examples of its type, an exhaustive dictionary of every species of magickal beast known to exist during the years it was written, most of which are no longer with us now. Those years were somewhere between 1097 and 1108, by the by, as near as we can judge. The last known copy of the book burned when Lord Torrant's library caught fire in 1907, taking the rest of the house with it. All we have left is a few sketch copies made by Torrant's secretary in 1904.

'Miranda will die,' I predicted. 'Of pure, unadulterated joy.'

'So will Val,' said Jay. 'But, Ves, it... it can't be Dramary's Bestiary, surely?'

'Why not? It looks like it.' I turned a few pages. I had seen the Torrant sketches before, and while I would need to see them again to make certain that they were a match for this book, I was fairly convinced. The style of the illustrations was very similar.

'Does nothing strike you as odd about this book?' said Jay.

'Besides its existence at all? Not really.'

'It's too new. Look at it.' Jay showed me its binding, which was, to be fair, unusually sound for a thousand year old book. The colours, too, were scarcely faded, and the ink still quite dark. It looked aged, but in a way that suggested it had been sitting on a shelf for a few centuries, not a millennium.

I exchanged a long, considering look with Jay, and some of Val's words floated back through my mind.

Earlier on, faced with the problem of risking a potentially fatal descent from the roof of the Striding Spire, or dying of exposure on top of it, I had not fully focused on everything that Val had said. But I did then.

There was the problem of the starstone, and the starstone Spire's apparent sightings well before that ought to have been possible.

There was the fact that the Spire itself had been spotted at various intervals down a number of centuries, though everything we had learned about it suggested it had only been built in the early seventeenth century.

There was Zareen's report about the Greyer cottage and its similar patterns of movement — and the fact that it had, to all appearances, been nowhere at all for considerable periods of time.

And then that book.

'My bag,' I said. 'I need Mauf.'

Jay pointed silently to the window, beneath which he had deposited my ever-present shoulder bag. I hauled Mauf out of it and said breathlessly: 'Mauf, those books and such you were canoodling with earlier. Did you get chance to, er, find out what they know?'

'I did not have full opportunity to absorb every word, Miss Vesper, but I believe I acquired the majority.'

'Magnificent you. Tell me one thing: is there anything in there to confirm when the building known as the Striding Spire was built?'

'There was not.'

My heart sank with disappointment.

'There was, however, reference to a building called the Starstone Spire, which was built in 1611.'

My heart almost stopped with excitement. 'Mauf! Who built it?'

'Its construction was ordered by Drystan Redclover, Mayor of Dappledok Dell, though it is noted that his brother Melmidoc was as active a participant in the process as the Mayor.'

'Jay,' I said, and my voice shook. 'In your Waymaster training, did you ever hear tell of a time when Waymasters could — could cross large expanses of time as well as distance?'

'Never.' Jay was clutching the Bestiary like it was his new born first child, and I noticed his hands were shaking too. 'Ves, if that was ever true, it would be the kind of discovery that... hell, it would set the world on fire.'

17

'Oh, it would,' I agreed. 'And that would give, for example, the Hidden Ministry strong reason to keep it secret, wouldn't you say?'

'No wonder Val had a hard time digging anything up.'

The pup jumped up onto one of the chairs and lay down in a cloud of dust. I could almost swear that she winked at me. 'The Greyer cottage. John Wester was a more powerful Waymaster even than we thought, Jay, for that cottage — it must have taken a jaunt back a few centuries, and quite recently.'

Jay eyed the sleepy pup with an air of dejection. 'And Zareen nuked it.'

'She is going to be gutted.'

'But the Spire?' Jay looked around at the room we were in, as though its décor might yield some manner of clue. 'It seems dead to me.'

'Long abandoned,' I agreed. 'Can you, I don't know, sense the presence of another Waymaster somehow?'

'How would I do that?'

I shrugged. 'Mauf, is there anything in those papers about how the Starstone Spire worked?'

'Or what it did?' put in Jay.

'Little that is likely to be of interest to you,' answered the book. 'Its recorded purpose was merely residential. It was a private project of the Redclover brothers, and its tendency to perambulate was only noted much later. And without the full approval of the Dappledok Councils.'

'There's no mention of its time-wandering capabilities?' I asked.

'None, but there are notes regarding its habit of disappearing without trace fairly often. I believe the writer assumed the Spire had simply gone to another Dell, or to somewhere in Britain. They may not have been aware of the possibility of an alternative.'

That was interesting. It implied that those brothers had developed the Spire's more remarkable capabilities themselves, privately, and without sharing it with the school or the town. Then again, why should they? Had we not already agreed that such powers would attract all kinds of attention, some of it very wrong indeed?

But what had happened to them?

The light dimmed momentarily, as though a cloud had crossed in front of the setting sun — or something moving much faster than that. I looked out of the window.

A trio of winged horses was on the approach. With the sun behind them, they were in silhouette, and I could not see who was riding them. 'I really hope this is Rob,' I said to Jay. 'Because I am starving.'

It wasn't Rob, but it was Zareen, and Miranda, and to my particular surprise, Baron Alban. It was the Baron who contrived to bring his steed up outside the window, and grinned in at us. 'Need a ride?'

'That, and dinner.'

He doffed his hat — a grey trilby, today — to me. 'Yours to command, my lady.'

We opted not to climb out of the window again, not when there were perfectly good stairs to be used. I took the pup under one arm, only to be immediately relieved of her by Miranda at the bottom, who gathered her up with a mother's tenderness and cooed something incomprehensible at her.

I realised, guiltily, that I had missed her last couple of feeds. I hoped Miranda would forgive me, considering the circumstances.

'You haven't been feeding her, have you?' said Miranda, fixing me with a gimlet eye.

So much for that. 'Yes!' I yelped. 'Except for the last few hours, but there was that whole stuck-on-the-roof thing, and we were distracted by...'

With a tut, Miranda walked off, already rummaging in her bag for a milk bottle.

'Dramary's Bestiary and time travel,' I finished.

The Baron grabbed me in a hug, the squeezy kind. '*Ves, you little vixen! Is it true?*'

'Er,' I choked. 'Cannot yet confirm, but all signs point to yes.'

Zareen punched the air. '*I knew it.*'

'Oh? Since when?'

'Since all that digging Val and I did. It didn't add up, unless you factor in possible time leaps.'

'Mauf's got some records stashed which we can go through for more detail,' I told her, tapping the Baron's head until he set me on my feet again. 'And there's a lot of books in there.'

Zareen nodded. 'Milady's sending an incursion, soon as I confirm we've got you.'

'How did you find us, anyway?'

'Iridescent water. That was a good tip. Val found a reference to a mermaid cove, and there's some old legend that says the waters turned pearly with the tears of some dumb princess or something. I daresay there's another explanation. You are in Nautilus Cove, in case you're interested, and it's sort of tucked into the Norfolk coast. Hi, Jay.'

Jay, engaged in stuffing Dramary's Bestiary (with great care) into my shoulder bag, merely nodded her way.

Zareen eyed the book hungrily. 'Is that really Dramary's Bestiary?'

'Seems to be,' said Jay.

Her fingers twitched. 'Damn it. I'm going to have to wait in line behind Mir, aren't I?'

'And Val, I should say.'

'And me,' said the Baron.

Zareen scowled at them both. 'I mean, I saved everybody's hide a fortnight ago with my amazing powers of exorcism, but sure. You can make me wait behind the Baron.'

'And destroyed the only building more or less known to be capable of time leaps,' said Jay, with a crooked smile.

'I did, didn't I?' groaned Zareen, and put her face in her hands.

Baron Alban gave the rump of his silver horse a friendly pat. 'Shall we go?'

I wanted to stay and read every word of every book in that library, of course, but I also really needed a plateful of crumpets and a bucket of tea. So I said, 'Tally ho,' and hopped up onto the Baron's horse. He mounted behind me, wound an arm around my waist, and nudged the beautiful creature into motion.

'Hold on tight,' he said in my ear.

Weary, cold and worn out with excitement, I had energy only to respond with a single syllable, and not even a meaningful one. 'Mm,' I said, at my most intelligent.

He chuckled. 'Hang in there, Ves. We'll get you fed shortly.'

'IT IS UNFORTUNATE,' SAID Milady the following day, 'that your findings were not more concrete. However, I have a few points of interest to share.'

Jay and I had returned Home to a fine feast of a dinner, and to my relief we had been permitted to spend the remainder of the evening recovering from our escapades, uninterrupted by any summons from Milady. She had even give us sufficient time, upon the following morning, to sleep in.

I felt loved.

At eleven sharp the next morning the summons had come, and by then I was more than ready to report, for I was dying of curiosity upon one or two points. House had provided chairs for us in Milady's tower, which was nice. I had bagsied the purple one and sat straight-backed therein, stubbornly resisting the temptation to sprawl out comfortably. It was that kind of chair. Jay had a plush red number to my right. Milady, as ever, was a sparkle in the air, and there was nobody else present.

It had not taken all that long to make our report, since much of its contents had already found its way to Milady via Valerie and Zareen. The bit about the Starstone Spire prompted a silence from Milady which I wanted to call enthralled, but which might rather have been grim.

'Firstly,' continued Milady, 'I have received an enquiry from the Hidden Ministry as to your doings and findings in Dappledok Dell. Naturally I returned a comprehensive answer, and have subsequently received a strict order of secrecy. No part of your discoveries, or any theories as to their possible meanings, are to be shared outside of this Society. Indeed, I have been strongly encouraged to refrain from mentioning it to anybody within the Society either, though they did not quite have the temerity to order my silence there as well.'

Interesting.

Jay gave a whistle. 'Sounds like we might be on to something.'

'I fear so, Jay.'

'Permission to keep digging?' I said hopefully.

'I am sorry, Ves, but no. Not at this time. And I hope this will not be one of those occasions when you take it upon yourself to skirt around my decision.'

I tried my best to look innocent, which was probably about as successful as all the other times. 'Would I?'

'Please refrain. You have too much common sense to imagine that it would be in any way wise. The Ministry is correct to fear the consequences of a general discovery of any of the Redclover brothers' more remarkable achievements.'

'But — but only imagine! Today, we are reduced to grubbing about in the dirt salvaging what little can be retrieved of a much-decayed heritage, and that's less and less every year. But if we could go back, nothing like Dramary's Bestiary need ever be lost again. No species will ever be extinct beyond revival, no great Treasures — the kinds that save lives, even! — will ever be destroyed or lost. We could do so much more good!'

'Yes, but for every advantage you could name, there is the less desirable alternative. Some Treasures are better lost, there is not room in this world for every magickal beast to survive, and while the Bestiary is a delight, it is still only a book. Time is cruel, Ves, but some of its more brutal effects are sadly necessary, however much we may wish it otherwise.'

I was too busy choking internally over the words "only a book" to reply. I was disappointed, too. Milady's arguments made sense overall, but the fact that they were coming from her made rather less. She could be a lot more rules-oriented than me, sure, but she was also extremely dedicated to the Society, and its goals. How could she flatly turn down such an opportunity?

'What if the wrong people got hold of a functional Striding Spire, or Greyers' Cottage?' said Jay, who obviously had more of his wits intact. 'What if Ancestria Magicka—' He came to an abrupt halt, his eyes wide.

'Precisely,' said Milady.

Oh.

Oh, dear.

I had wondered before what was the real purpose behind Ancestria Magicka. On the face of it, they were doing the same kinds of things as we were, albeit with different motives. Tracking down lost artefacts and retrieving them, restoring them, saving them — whatever you wanted to call it. Their ultimate intentions might be more materialistic than altruistic, but it was essentially the same gig. We weren't the only two such organisations in Britain, either, not to mention the rest of the world.

But someone had gone to enormous trouble and expense to found Ancestria Magicka, very recently. Emphasis on the expense. They had been kitted out with the very best of everything and everyone — and why? I wasn't exaggerating when I said there was less and less left of our magickal heritage to salvage. Could they hope to find enough valuable Treasures to justify the extraordinary amounts of money they were shelling out? Either they were confident that they could, somehow, or they were being backed by somebody with oodles of money to burn, and no particular concern how much of it they lost.

If the former... how were they so confident they could do better than we could? The Society was founded eons ago, it had many years of experience behind it, and while it wasn't nearly so well-funded as Ancestria Magicka, it still managed to attract many top professionals in our shared field. We did well.

And we still didn't get hold of anywhere near enough valuables to cover our costs, even had we been disposed to sell them, which wasn't at all the point.

What if we were not the first people in modern history to rediscover the Redclover brothers and their Striding Spire? Or what if somebody had stumbled over the Greyer Cottage, or a similar example?

That would be a pretty strong motive for somebody moneyed and ambitious to go all-in at this game. And Ancestria Magicka had sent some of their best agents out in pursuit of the Greyer Cottage, with the apparent goal of coercing its resident spirits into working for their organisation instead. We had assumed that all they wanted was to set up their headquarters, Ashdown Castle, as an equivalent to our own, dear House — with extra perambulatory capabilities as a bonus. But what if they had known more than we did? What if they had actually been after John Wester because he was the only surviving (more or less) Waymaster who could leap through time, as well as space?

Hang on, though. What if John Wester wasn't the only one left? What if there were more?

'Um,' I said, and swallowed something like bile. 'What else do they know that we do not?'

'Too much,' said Milady grimly. 'And I am sorry to add that Lord Garrogin's hunt for a double agent has ended in failure. According to his conclusions, no one at Home was responsible for feeding information about the book to Ancestria Magicka, or for secreting a tracking enchantment between its pages. This means either that someone anticipated his involvement, and has contrived a way to lie successfully even to a Truthseeker, or that there is some other explanation, the details of which I cannot begin to guess.'

'That's a problem,' I said weakly.

'Zareen, I am afraid to say, came under particularly close scrutiny, considering her apparent prior acquaintance with George Mercer.'

'It cannot have been Zar,' I said quickly.

'I believe it to be most unlikely myself,' said Milady. 'The worst I am inclined to believe is that she may, in an unguarded moment, have let something slip about the book. But that she would go to the lengths of compromising its security, I am much more in doubt. However.'

I did not like the way Milady said *however*. Her voice had gone all cold.

'If she indeed has connections with a member of an opposing organisation, whose motives and possible information we have increasing reason to fear, then those connections must be put to use for the benefit of the Society. I do not believe either of you will much like the next assignment I have in mind for you, but you must accept my apologies.'

I now understood what Mabyn had meant when she had described Milady as *apologetic, but not at all sorry*. 'Anything you require of us shall of course be carried out, Milady,' I said as stoutly as I could.

'I know, Ves,' she replied. 'I need you to find out the nature of Zareen's acquaintance with Mercer, and how close they are. I also need you to ascertain the extent of Zareen's loyalty to the Society.'

'I don't need to do that last part,' I said. 'I know her to be entirely loyal.'

'Would you stake your life on it, my Ves?'

'Without hesitation.' Zareen has been a member of the Society for almost as long as I have, and she has always had my back. I have always had hers. I could not doubt her, any more than I could doubt my left arm or my right leg.

Jay shifted in his seat, but thankfully said nothing.

Milady was silent for a time.

'Zareen has told me that she met Mercer at school,' Milady finally said. 'And that there is little contact between them now. I hope the latter is not quite true, for we *must* learn what the group calling themselves Ancestria Magicka know, and with minimal further loss of time. If, as we fear, they are ahead of us in the matter of the Spire, or other, equivalent resources, they must be interfered with before they have chance to do anything too damaging with this dangerous knowledge. Your assignment, then, is as follows.'

Milady can be the queen of dramatic pauses, when she wants to. Jay and I waited. I, at least, might have been holding my breath.

'I require you to go renegade,' said Milady in a dispassionate tone. 'To my infinite regret, my two best Acquisitions Specialists and I have been unable to agree regarding your recent findings, and the three of us have parted ways. Zareen shall join you. Your goal is to found a more forward-thinking establishment, without me and my hidebound, restrictive notions. You will leave this House tomorrow morning with everything you can carry, and no more. Temporary accommodation will be provided for you. Your contact will be Rob, who, poor man, cannot at all decide whether he would like to remain with the Society or join in with your exciting new adventure. Others may secretly offer you what aid they may. I imagine my recent decisions may prove sadly unpopular with all manner of my employees.'

I, too dumbfounded to speak, could only nod. Jay said nothing either.

Milady's middle name had better be "Devious", or I shall be sorely disappointed.

'This news shall of course reach Ancestria Magicka by way of Zareen and George Mercer,' continued Milady. 'I shall be most interested to know what their response to it will prove to be.'

I found my voice. 'To be clear, Milady. Are we to actually pursue any of these fictional goals during our sojourn away from Home?'

'That I leave in your capable hands, Ves. Yours too, Jay. I am sure you will know just how to proceed.'

In other words, Milady could not officially tell us to investigate the Spire, or the Greyer Cottage, any further. If it were known that she had done so, the future of the entire Society could be at risk — being, as we are, dependent upon the Ministry's goodwill, not to mention funding.

But she could no more ignore this development than we could. The alternative, then? Put us in a position where we could do it without, apparently, her official sanction, and she could deny all knowledge of it later.

That put us in an interesting predicament, for if the Hidden Ministry found out what we were up to, it would be more difficult for Milady, no longer our employer, to shield us from the consequences.

On the other hand, for a little while we had more or less total freedom to do as we chose. Dangerous or not, that was going to be a hell of a lot of fun.

Jay, though, was struggling. 'Is... um, does this amount to official permission to...?'

'No,' said Milady.

'It amounts to unofficial permission,' said I.

The sparkle in the air brightened for a moment, which I had always taken to be Milady's way of laughing at us. Nicely, of course. 'Listen to Ves,' she told Jay. 'Do as she thinks best. She will not lead you too far astray.'

'Or at least, not much farther than is justifiable,' I amended. And considering that we had just been given an unofficial order to kick over pretty much all the traces, quite a lot was going to be justifiable.

'Dismissed, then,' said Milady. 'There's chocolate in the pot, and you may take the pot with you when you leave.'

I heaved a small, inward sigh of relief. To brave the dangers of the Ministry, Ancestria Magicka, the Spire and clear and consistent misdemeanour all at once was one thing. To do it without a drop of Milady's finest hot chocolate was quite another.

'Stop by Zareen's on your way down,' added Milady. 'You will find her reasonably well-informed already.'

'THIS IS NOT WHAT I had in mind when I joined the Society,' said Jay a short while later.

We were huddled up in Zareen's tiny cubbyhole of a room, what we colloquially call the Toil and Trouble division. We were sharing the chocolate three ways, Zareen in her big chair with her feet on the desk, Jay and I perching on the edges of the latter.

'You thought it would be straightforward, did you?' said Zareen, without much sympathy.

'It was when my parents worked here,' he said, rather defensively.

'Division?' said Zareen.

'Enchantments, and Beasts.'

Zareen waved a hand dismissively. 'Tame stuff. Welcome to Acquisitions and Research. Much more fun.'

'Much more confusing,' said Jay.

I felt some sympathy for him, I really did. He was the type to prefer to play by the rules. It made him feel better. What was he supposed to do with a job where the rules changed by the day, and where you could be officially (unofficially) ordered to ignore them all? He wasn't going to find it easy.

'We'll make a maverick of you yet,' I said to him, with a reassuring pat to his shoulder.

'Great,' he muttered.

'So let's get this straight,' said Zareen, finishing her chocolate with an appreciative slurp and setting her empty cup upon the desk. 'We're to sort of found our own Society splinter group, independent of Milady's authority or influence, with some degree of help from supposed rogue agents within the Society. I'm to make George believe we've gone rebel, in case Ancestria wants to take another shot at recruiting us, and if they do, we're to find out what they know about the Spire — and anything else we can dig up, too. Oh, and if we can manage to find out how the Spire worked, and whether there are any more functional examples left in the world, then we get bonus points.'

'That's pretty much it,' I said. 'Oh — if we can find another Dappledok pup, too, Miranda will love us forever. She wants a breeding pair.'

'The Ministry might have let us keep the current one, but they'll never go for our having a breeding pair.'

'Milady will talk them round. Or ignore them.'

Jay snorted.

Zareen silently checked about twelve things off on her fingers. 'Right. Easy,' she said, with a roll of her eyes, and reached for her phone.

'So how do you know George Mercer?' I put in, as she waited for whoever it was to pick up.

'Met him at the School of Weird.'

'The what?'

'The Seminary for the Stranger Arts. Already an adorable euphemism. They mean the Dark and Dire Arts of course, but nobody quite went for that title for some reason. The students call it the School of Weird. Oh,' she said then into her phone. 'Hi, darling. We need to talk. Usual place? Great. Tonight, eight o'clock.' She hung up.

'George?' I guessed.

She nodded.

So much for little real contact between them. But then, Milady had probably known that. Zar didn't hobnob with George Mercer in the same way that she and Jay and I were in no way sallying forth to disobey all the Ministry's sternest orders with Milady's semi-official sanction.

'Excellent,' I said to Zareen. 'Can we come?'

'No.'

'Please?'

A pause, and a glare from Zareen. 'Oh, fine,' she said, capitulating with a sigh. 'I never could resist the Ves puppy eyes for long.'

I grinned smugly. 'I know.'

Also By Charlotte E. English

Modern Magick

The Road to Farringale

Toil and Trouble

The Striding Spire

The Fifth Britain

Royalty and Ruin

Music and Misadventure

The Wonders of Vale

The Heart of Hyndorin

Alchemy and Argent
The Magick of Merlin
Dancing and Disaster

House of Werth

Wyrde and Wayward
Wyrde and Wicked
Wyrde and Wild